Locker 572

a novel

D1456187

LT KoDZo

Locker 572

© 2011, 2014, 2016 ,2019 by LT Kodzo. All rights reserved.

This fourth edition published by Kodzo Books, www.kodzobooks.com.

Cover design by The Cover Collection

Font 'Passing Notes' created by http://bythebutterfly.com

ISBN-13: 978-1-943960-31-6
ISBN-10: 194396031X

"I read this book as part of my review of appropriate materials for my work in statewide suicide prevention. I asked my colleagues, staff and college-aged children to do the same. We all agreed that this was a riveting, well-written book, presented in the "kids' vernacular" so that youth can easily relate to this book. It was thoroughly researched and used correct, sensitive language that will not be offensive to those of us who have lost loved ones to suicide. ... I plan to use it as a resource in a graduate course I teach on suicide prevention."

Melanie Puorto Conte
NY State, Suicide Prevention Director

"Great book! This book will capture your attention from the first page and keep it throughout the novel. ... This book is timely and relevant to today's world. It touches on three topics close to my heart; foster care, suicide and bullying.... This book is a must read for all teachers, school administrators, social workers, foster and adoptive parents, preteens, teenagers and anyone else who works with children from preschool through high school age."

Bruce Sharp
Tenured Foster Care Worker

Chapter 1

Sheridan shouldered past an anorexic brunette with a ponytail.

"Hey! What do you think you're doing?" a mean-faced girl shouted.

"This is none of your business," another said.

Sheridan ignored them and focused on their victim. "Are you okay?" Her last fight had been with a boy in Yuba County her junior year. Beat the snot out of him. She didn't like confrontation, but she hated bullies more. "Do you need help?"

Instead of gratitude, fear filled the small girl's eyes. "Leave me alone."

"You heard her, skank."

"Yeah, take your noisy butt back to the crack house you came from."

Sheridan faced her challengers. The four Barbies created a wall between Sheridan and the thankless girl as if they were now protecting her. The terrorized kid might not be thankful, but she wasn't stupid. With her tormentors now focused on Sheridan, the girl slipped away. Purpose accomplished.

Lame as it was to start a new school this way, Sheridan couldn't ignore the harassment. "Ladies." Sheridan dusted her hands. The doors to North Harbor High waited over their thin shoulders. Seven more months to graduation. Despite what just happened, she didn't want any trouble. The drones circled her as the queen bee stepped forward and slapped Sheridan.

"Who do you think you are?"

A second girl spat at her.

Pulling back every defensive urge in her gut, Sheridan silently wiped off the snotty saliva. The swarm hovered. Shoulders pulled back, she focused on the school entrance and stepped forward.

With a couple of shoves they let her pass.

"Courtney, check out those boots."

"The Salvation Army must be having a sale."

Their attempts to humiliate strengthened Sheridan's pace. They'd picked on the one thing she wasn't ashamed of. Her footwear.

"Wait! I've seen those boots before." Her new fans followed her inside.

"Yeah, on a hooker." The two-dimensional twits cackled and fell all over each other with that one.

Inside the school the heels of her knee-length black leathers clicked on the faux marble of the building foyer. She hummed a little of "These Boots Are Made for Walkin'," the original Nancy Sinatra version. Much cooler than any remake.

A cop leaned against the brick wall. The gang elbowed past her with whispered threats of "later," and then disappeared around a corner. Sheridan puffed out a breath. The rest of her senior year would happen here. The first period bell hadn't even rung yet and she'd broken the first rule on her list: stay out of trouble. Whatever. Better to act than ignore. Nothing to do but move forward. Focus on rule number two: graduate.

A couple doorbell tones sounded from the speakers. This school was huge. Students of all sizes and shapes pushed and shoved in waves. Even the tall ceilings were strangely suffocating. The good air floated up high out of reach. She stopped a boy who looked ten and asked, "Can you tell me where Miss Leslie Jones' office is?"

"Second floor." His deep voice didn't fit his little body.

"Thanks."

Sheridan climbed the wide staircase. The shuffle of feet got louder. Halls cleared. Group noise lowered to random voices and died into silence as she found the door marked *Office.*

Here goes.

She pulled open the door and peeked inside. The room was lyrical. Books lined shelves unevenly yet balanced like notes on a sheet of paper. Further inside the old pane-style windows released from the top and bottom. One open window let in a breeze. A wind chime read the music of the room.

"Can I help you?" a studious girl in a vintage brown cardigan asked from the other side of a small desk.

"Yes. I'm looking for Leslie Jones."

"What's your name?"

"Sheridan Alexander."

"Do you have an appointment?" The girl's expression remained indifferent behind her thick-rimmed glasses.

Would she need ten forms of ID to get in? "Yes. I'm transferring."

The girl got up and said, "Walk this way."

Sheridan followed, limping like Igor in the cult classic *Young Frankenstein*. The girl turned around. Sheridan jerked to a stop then smiled without showing her teeth. The aide didn't smile back. Sheridan shrugged her eyebrows and entered the room at the end of the corridor.

"Have a seat." The counselor pointed across the messy room without looking up. If the reception area was musical, this office was noisy. Paper cluttered the desk and walls and shelves. Some files attempted to escape a gray metal cabinet like people from a tall building on fire. Others lay limp on the floor. The only clean spot in the room was an oversized armchair. Sheridan eased herself into it.

"Hi, I'm Miss Jones." The counselor's curly red hair chaotically framed a freckled face. The clothes she wore looked outdated and yet hip at the same time, while bangles and necklaces littered her body. "Sorry for the mess." The words hung like a how-are-you-I-am-fine greeting. "My job generates plenty of paperwork."

Sheridan lifted the corners of her mouth.

"Let me get your file." With a magician's skill, the counselor slipped a blue folder from a tall stack without knocking it over. "Sheridan Alexander. Am I right?"

"Yes." Not profound. How many transfer students could there be in November?

"Looks like this isn't your first move." Miss Jones flipped a page without looking up. "Your fifth foster home since kindergarten." Unlike other people who knew, the counselor stated it as a simple fact. Sheridan liked her for that. "Now, that's a lot of paperwork."

Sheridan had met her type before. The foster system had more than a handful of dot-the-i-cross-the-t type of adults who used paperwork to control the world. Rules and boundaries were cool, as long as they applied equally to everyone.

"Now, this late in the year, we don't usually have open lockers." The grown-up twisted some of her bracelets. "And the rules say only freshmen are supposed to share. As a senior, I don't want to squeeze you in with one of them."

The counselor paused. Sheridan didn't rescue her. The system taught her how to sit in an office for hours and be silent.

"There is *one* locker that recently became vacant."

The counselor broke eye contact and tapped her fingers on the file. An ugly gray hummingbird with a blood-red neck hovered near the windowsill. There were no flowers or feeders nearby. He bounced up and down in the air as if trying to get Sheridan's attention. The bird's frantic wings matched Sheridan's heart rate.

"It's not in the best shape, but the janitors will clean it up." Miss Jones stopped again as if she'd run out of words. The bird was gone.

"I'm sure it will be okay." Sheridan donated a comment to shake off the heebees.

"Well, I'd rather you take a look." The counselor passed her a crisp piece of paper. "It's a map of the school. I've written the locker number and combination on top. We can walk you through your schedule when you return. Take this pass with you." She held out a red plastic card attached to a string. Sheridan reluctantly hung it around her neck. The stupid thing might as well have bells on it. "Come back here after you've checked it out."

"Sure." Sheridan shook out the school map even though it wasn't wrinkled. Next to the locker number was its three digit combination. According to the diagram, 572 was located in the basement. Not a good sign.

In the vacant hall she tiptoed to the stairs because the loud click of her boots ricocheted off the walls. Whatever was sleeping, she didn't want to wake it. The old building had classroom doors with windows. The students sat in their places with bright, shiny faces. Sheridan tried not to compare them to zombies.

The foreboding didn't ease when she reached the lowest level. The overhead lights were not the fluorescent kind from upstairs. Instead, abandoned bulbs littered the ceiling with random empty sockets. Buried one level below ground, she turned left at the end of the hall, wishing she was back upstairs. She'd rather watch students half alive than this dead-end hall of fifty or so lockers. They were different from the thin, modern cabinets upstairs. The metal doors were wide and squatty like tombs. The further she descended, the darker it got. The bulbs at the end of the row were broken or burnt-out.

And what was that smell? Number 572 was more than disgusting. It reeked. Sheridan pulled her shirt over her face and held it there with her hand. The ghosts of obscenities hid beneath a single layer of white paint. The most visible insult carved into the metal was "ring around the toilet." Fresh paint flaked around the words.

"Wow." This locker could actually be contagious. "No wonder it's available." Fifty kids in one hundred would have given up at that moment, but Sheridan hated being average. The knob felt greasy in her hand. With a tissue from her oversized purse she twisted the combination, pinched the handle, and lifted up. As soon as the door opened, fumes assaulted her from something old and moldy inside.

She held her breath. The hazardous smell attacked her stomach. Egg shells and orange peels and any other food substance that would fit through the vents covered the inside of the locker. Dried milk and soda streaked the back of the door like modern art.

"No way. It would be better to share with a freshman."

But as she slammed the door closed, a white item in the litter caught her eye. Unless she was wrong, something sweet lay on top of the stinky mess. She hustled into the more open hallway to catch her breath.

What a joke. A school locker was her home away from foster care. The kids in this school were ruthless. No doubt the work of the shakedown crew from this morning. So, who would slip something delicate into a locker everyone else mucked up? She wasn't convinced it would be worth it, but she had to go back and make sure.

With a couple of deep breaths and her mouth double-covered, Sheridan went back to the locker. It took three tries before she got the combination right. The door swung open. The smell wasn't as bad. She kept her nose pinched and breathed through her mouth. Trash men didn't die from inhaling this stuff, did they?

The grossness was worth it because her eyes hadn't lied to her. Delicate and soft, resting on top of the rubble was of all things a daisy. Wild. She rescued the blossom between pinched fingers. Why would someone put a flower into a trashed locker? Why would anyone trash a locker in the first place?

She slammed the door shut and rushed to the open hallway for more oxygen. The limp petals lay lifeless in her hand. A couple years on the farm taught her growing things have seasons. Flowers grow in the spring not late fall. But San Diego was different from up North. One old song on her playlist claimed "It Never Rains in Southern California." Maybe flowers grew out of season as well.

Either way, this summer symbol didn't fit the school. The flower had been inserted recently. The fragile petals bent in her palm. She hurried back to the metal door, convinced she'd keep the locker. The stem fit into the vent like an expensive vase. Now the daisy was on display. The flower had a story, and she needed to uncover it.

Chapter 2

The lock on the darkroom door jiggled.

Crackers!

Ashley Nobel dropped the photo onto the table and struggled out of her gloves. The sound of metal against metal meant the person on the other side of the door had a key. She ran to the door and pushed her whole weight against it as the bolt began to twist.

"Wait!" she shouted, holding the knobbed lock in place. The rest of her life would be disastrous if the gang discovered Ashley's work in the old darkroom.

"Who's in there?"

"Ashley." Behind her, six photographs of Ribbon Barber dripped from a clothesline. And the seventh lay wet on the table where she dropped it. Of the twenty-four prints, these screamed betrayal. She shouldn't have said her stupid name.

"Why didn't you turn on the warning light?" Only ten other kids had a key.

"I forgot." She flipped the switch. Most of North Harbor ignored the light bulb next to the darkroom door. Kids wanting the technical drawing class across the hall walked in when the light was on. The lock protected negatives better. "Give me fifteen minutes."

"Fine. Turn off the light when you're done." Students had strict instructions to share the room. And on any other day she would have let him in.

"Yeah, okay." Ashley hugged the door. Her jaw stopped gnawing on the ever-present gum. She listened with her ear pressed against the wood until she was sure the student on the other side had walked away.

The brightest part of Ashley's day happened within these painted black walls. And she wasn't even emo. The acidic odor of the chemical process inspired her. She enjoyed seeing an image in its black-and-white negative. People appeared inside-out, their sinister souls exposed. Her problem now — prints took hours to dry. She'd planned the entire lunch hour to develop these shots. That was reduced to minutes. The teacher warned them a blow dryer could ruin the prints. But so what? The risk of water spots and dust was better than getting caught as a sympathizer. Any connection to Ribbon Barber was a death sentence at North Harbor High.

She scrambled through her gym bag. The cord to her dryer became tangled with her flat iron and a random shoelace. Ashley didn't have time to untangle the mess. She dragged the entire jumble to an outlet in the corner and plugged in the cord for the dryer. If it ruined them, it ruined them. She had no choice. That kid would check out whatever she left behind. He'd blab it around school. In fact, it would be hot gossip to link Ashley to the most hated girl in school, even if Ribbon used to be her friend. Well, especially because Ribbon used to be her friend. That secret must never come out.

Ashley picked up the first photo of the rejected girl and carried it over to the dryer. The whirr of hot air echoed through the room. Taking Ribbon's picture was dumb. The girl should have fought back. Nobody likes a wimp. The whole thing was stupid.

The water trickled off the print in tears. Each photo dried faster than she imagined. Ashley placed each dried photo between two pages in her folder. The strong drive to protect these prints wasn't purely selfish. Courtney and the gang would turn them into something vulgar. If only Ribbon were around. The film had been in her camera bag for exactly fourteen days. Ashley didn't mean to count, but it was so odd.

The day after the pictures were taken Ribbon just up and disappeared. That was two weeks ago.

Ashley stuffed her things into her gym bag. She'd shove it into her locker before joining the gang for lunch. With a couple minutes to spare, she pulled back the curtain, turned off the warning light, and unlocked the door. It wouldn't matter if anyone saw her leave, now the evidence was safely buried.

The tech center hallway was empty. She adjusted her camouflage. Not the forest green or desert tan of war, but the popular Old Navy tee and True Religion jeans worn on the high school battlefield. As she headed for the main building, a breeze across the football field whispered to her. Stop thinking of Ribbon. The girl was Courtney's longest running target. The only kid who got assaulted *every* day.

The lunchroom contained its typical subgroups. Courtney and the crew occupied the center table. They gossiped about some new kid. The gang had become a pack of rabid dogs since Ribbon's disappearance. They drooled at the thought of fresh meat. According to the troupe, the girl started school in a pair of knee-high leather boots and a backpack full of attitude. Whoever this new girl was, she'd better be strong.

Ashley squeezed in between Maddie and another wannabe. Courtney, Ashley, and Helen started the group in junior high. Now there were at least twelve true princesses and an entire school of scared commoners. Last year the whole thing became lame to Ashley. Too vulgar and pubescent. Ashley looked into Courtney's envy-colored eyes. They matched her personality the way her shoes matched her purse.

Nauseated by the cafeteria's idea of spaghetti, Ashley pushed it away.

"I don't want that," Maddie gasped at the tray that now sat in front of her.

"I never said you did." Ashley outranked the girl. Courtney proved this by tilting her head toward the plate drop-off center. Maddie obediently hurried the still full plate to the dishwashers. The group would never think Ashley's loss of appetite had anything to do with guilt. They counted calories the way nerds monitored their GPA.

"Check out Courtney's new ring," Helen bragged for the leader. "Her dad bought it while he was overseas. An actual emerald from Ireland. Can you believe it?"

The grassy stone glowed from a platinum band before it winked at her like a disgusting pervert. "That's great." Ashley twirled the small pearl on her pinkie. It was the only real gem she owned, but now it felt small. Courtney was good at making other people's joy seem trivial. Once Ashley got home she'd pack the junior high school gift in a drawer. It couldn't embarrass her there.

"Did you go by locker 572 today?" Courtney moved from sitting on top of the table to the seat across from

Ashley.

"No, why should I?" If the self-appointed leader of the school found out Ashley was tired of the petty gossip and trash talk, she'd be toast.

"Some idiot put a daisy in the vent of Ribbon's old locker."

"A what?" Ashley swallowed her gum.

"An eff-ing daisy," Helen practically shouted.

"Like a flower?" Ashley tried to keep calm.

"Can you believe it?" Courtney leaned against the table.

That was the last thing Ashley needed. First the photos, now this. She was close to positive she pushed the flower all the way into the locker's vents yesterday. A private message from Ashley to Ribbon. Who moved it? No one else at North Harbor knew the love-me-love-me-not flower was Ribbon's favorite. Nobody even talked to the girl.

"Why would someone do that?" Ashley asked.

"Who cares?" Helen clicked her tongue. The twit had been trying to take Ashley's position for more than a year. The poser copied Courtney's style from her painted toes to the same brand of lip gloss. "Maybe it means 'rest in peace.'" While everyone laughed at Helen's joke, Ashley lifted her lips in a fake smile.

She wanted the food tray back. It would give her something to mess with. Ashley reached into her purse for a fresh piece of gum and changed the dangerous subject. "What were you saying about a new girl?"

"She's so last year," Courtney answered.

Puppet-head Helen agreed. "Her boots are out-of-date knock-offs."

Ashley tried not to gag on the artificial sweetener

coming from both Helen and her gum. It would be so nice to spend one lunch break not tearing people down. There had to be a cafeteria somewhere in the world where people talked about the weather. Before the girls could continue bashing the short blonde with an outdated pixie, Maddie came running back.

"Ribbon's definitely gone." Maddie was out of breath.

"Yeah?" Courtney beamed like her boyfriend had just won a soccer match.

"After I dropped off the tray, I decided to take Ashley's pudding and pour it into Ribbon's locker." She stopped long enough to make eye contact with each girl in the circle. "The janitor is cleaning it out."

"They do that once a month." Courtney shrugged. She'd spent the first year making sure she got a legion of kids involved in terrorizing Ribbon's locker. The custodians couldn't keep up. Since September, locker 572 was cleaned monthly.

"Nope." Maddie's ponytail swatted the air as she shook her head. "They're painting it and everything."

"Maybe she transferred." Ashley crossed imaginary fingers hoping Ribbon's two-week absence meant the girl found the guts to escape. About time.

"Whatever," Helen said. "Ribbon's gone for good."

"The school smells better already." Courtney stood and led the crew out of the cafeteria. Maddie giggled. Ashley gnawed on her gum. Her allegiance had changed. She hadn't just avoided the group and changed her schedule—two weeks ago she supported the enemy.

Five steps out of the lunchroom, Courtney pointed out the new kid. The girl looked like Tinkerbell without the cocktail dress. Helen was wrong. The boots were actually nice. A little over-dressed for high school, but honestly, why should that matter? Who gets to decide? It wasn't the first time Ashley wondered who crowned Courtney queen of North Harbor High. If college was anything like high school, Ashley would rather serve burgers at McDonald's. In two years when she graduated, Ashley would erase her past and start over.

"Let's give her a nice welcome at the end of the day," Helen suggested.

"Yeah." Courtney laughed. "A little orientation."

Ashley passed. "I've got to get home and catch up on homework."

"You haven't been around lately." Courtney folded her arms.

"I'm grounded," Ashley lied.

"For what?" Helen butted in.

"An F in Civics." Ashley hated responding to Helen, but she'd rather do that than participate in whatever hazing they had planned.

"I'll text you later." Courtney made it sound more like a threat than a comment.

Chapter 3

The image of the daisy tugged at Sheridan all day. She didn't want to remember her last foster home or what caused the state to release her and the five other kids. But the injustice done to locker 572 yanked her back to events on the farm.

The grown-ups pulled the disgusting dad from the system. Big deal, he wouldn't foster any more children. But what if he decided to steal them? Nobody listened to her when she asked that question. He deserved nothing short of an operation. They neutered dogs, didn't they? Due to the controversy, the authorities divided up the litter and spread the kids out across the state of California like motherless mutts.

Adults were pointless in a crisis. Today, the teachers conspired against her. She'd planned to watch the janitor transform her new locker, but no.

"Miss Alexander, come to my desk after class to get some consent forms."

"Sheridan, before you leave I need to talk to you."

"Here's the homework you missed."

"Visit the counselor's office at lunch."

Were they kidding? By the time she finished her last class, she had a backpack full of books and papers. Typical. What did it matter now? School was over. She shouldered her load and said *"Au revoir"* to her French teacher.

The laughter in the hall irritated her. Sheridan pushed through the crowd. No one could stop her from going to locker 572 now. In the throng of North Harbor students, she hadn't made one friend. Not that she tried. She preferred eclectics over fakers, like the former owner of her new locker or at least the daisy-dropper. Sheridan searched the current of students streaming through the hallway; each drip looked like the next.

The phone in her backpack danced to Tex's achy-breaky ringtone. She dropped her fifty-pound school luggage to the floor.

"What?"

"Whoa." Her former foster-brother's drawl was thick. It wasn't real, which made it sometimes comedic. The black city boy with a silver-dollar belt buckle and matching cowboy hat wasn't Southern. He'd spent his entire life in California. All foster kids coped. Sheridan collected shoes and Tex used a cartoon accent. "Whatcha biting me fer?"

"I'm tired of people today, Tex."

"Then later, 'gator."

"No, wait." Sheridan heaved her pack onto her shoulder. Tex was the best brother she'd ever had. They both arrived at the farm their first year of high school. Her cowboy buddy was a wiz on the computer. Before they left Yuba County, he printed flyers of the old man and the crimes he'd done. Together they stapled them on every wooden pole on Marysville Road. It wouldn't erase the memories little Elsie would have her whole life. But it was more than the grown-ups did.

"So, what're they like?"

"Total jerks." Students ruled this hate-fest. Teachers didn't seem any better.

"Your new Ma and Pa?"

"Nina and Joe?" She shook her head to shuffle her brain.

"Yeah. You say they're jerks?"

"No. I was talking about the kids at school. The new foster parents are fine. A couple do-gooders."

"Ain't all foster folks?"

"Very funny." Sheridan switched the phone to her other ear. "This couple believes they are going to save my life with charts and graphs."

"Shoot. Is that all?"

"Why? What are yours like?" Sheridan weaved around students who refused to move for her. At the top of the stairs she stopped in a corner and dropped her backpack. For the first time all day, the locker could wait. Tex was her rare sense of belonging. She listened to his voice and let the rush of North Harbor blow past her.

"They actually track me with GPS."

"That sucks. Dude, we need to get out of this system."

The front-step Barbies appeared on the stairs below her. Sheridan straightened her short frame. "Look, can I call you back?"

"You betcha."

"Great." Sheridan flipped her phone closed and tucked it into the side pocket of her backpack. Two steroid-enhanced boys sauntered up the steps. The jocks yanked on their jerseys, gave a smug nod then climbed the steps two at a time. The ponytail started to follow the boys upstairs until the queen bee shot her an angry glance. Some species eat their young. Apparently, this group was one of them. The cluster of girls giggled and focused on the guys while Sheridan slipped past the clique.

She rounded the last flight and puffed out a heavy breath. Restraint wasn't her best quality. Quite the opposite. As she reached the basement she felt proud of herself. She'd resisted the urge to deck every one of them.

The basement had lost its dark and creepy aura. Missing light bulbs had been replaced. The heels of her boots clicked as the few remaining students slammed doors and scrambled from the building. She loved her shoes. All of them. They'd become home to more than her feet. She could depend on her footwear. The soft leather conformed to her foot like nothing else in life.

The daisy was gone. Number 572 had a fresh coat of paint. The nasty odor had lost its battle against the scent of pine. Sheridan twisted the lock. The disgusting mess from this morning was gone. The paint felt sticky, but almost dry. The garbage inside had been replaced with tree-shaped air fresheners. Three of them hung on the coat hooks. Sheridan had to give props to the poor guy who cleaned this up.

A stack of textbooks remained on the top shelf. Biology, Math and... wait a minute. The locker wasn't scrubbed of all mystery. A journal peeked out from under the books. Interesting. The locker still had secrets. She reached to grab it when she noticed the girls from upstairs. They loitered at the end of the hall, watching her.

For the first time all day, Sheridan wished she'd worn her knee-top Converse. Rubber soles would give her tired legs a better chance at freedom. Her only escape route would be through the hags. But not in these heels.

She faced the locker and slipped the journal off the shelf without removing any of the textbooks. It better be worth the beatdown she was about to get. She couldn't afford a suspension. Before she mapped out her full defense, an object whizzed across the hall. She ducked before it hit her head. A plastic bottle crashed against the wall behind her. Tomato juice splattered against her skin.

"Are you serious?" The plastic V-8 container spun on the floor next to her foot. These fools didn't know she'd spent the end of summer tossing fifty-pound bales of hay with Tex. If they wanted to tangle with her, no problem. She dropped the journal on the floor of the locker and covered it with her coat. She could do some serious damage.

Red fluid dripped from her hair as the group approached her. Sheridan tapped the tip of her boot and waited. There were six of them. She'd start with the leader. Scenarios played out in her mind. No matter how she calculated it, every situation would get her in trouble. Except restraint. Don't blow it on a bunch of juice-tossing idiots. She had to stay cool and get out of here. Tex would tell her these cows weren't worth wrestling. In the end, the grown-ups would blame the foster kid.

The gang surrounded her. Whatever happened, she wanted to make sure of two things. One, keep the journal; and two, don't fight back. Make sure these heifers had nothing to report to a teacher, principal, or parent. Sheridan turned to close the locker when someone grabbed her hair. Her quick reflexes helped her get a hand to her scalp. It took all the strength she had to not retaliate. She waited for the punches that didn't come. Instead, a quick shove from behind forced her face first inside the locker wall. Almost-dry paint stuck to her fingers as she tried to regain her balance. Unseen hands lifted her legs and tucked her into the locker.

"Welcome to North Harbor High, tramp." The door slammed.

Curled up like a pretzel, Sheridan shouted at them. "Sure, shove the short girl into the locker, very original." Her voice reverberated around her as the lock spun shut. Their laughter died away. They left her alone and in the dark. The antique basement lockers were wider than most, but the space was still tight. Her right hand was trapped between her leg and the wall. Who could she call? Not Nina and Joe. No way. There had to be someone else. Maybe the school office.

It wasn't until she heard Tex's achy-breaky ringtone through painted metal that she realized it would be impossible to call anyone. Her backpack didn't make it inside. At least the idiots who stuffed her into number 572 didn't chuck it into the trash.

Her wedged-in right shoulder ached. A little twist put her at an awkward, but less painful, angle. With her right knee in her face and her left one tucked under her, she managed to unzip one of her boots. She peeled the boot down her calf. With her foot free, she had three inches to maneuver her left leg into a full tucked position. She released the other boot and hung them on a hook over her head.

The corner of the journal poked into her butt. She wiggled her toes and twisted the book along the locker wall until she could prop it up on her knees. The vents at the top of the locker didn't provide enough light to read, but the penlight on her keys would.

Regular kids would be worried about how long they might be imprisoned in a locker. But they didn't live in foster care. This was nothing. Sheridan lifted her elbow up high enough to get two fingers into the pocket under her foot. She dug until she could pinch the rubber smiley face between them. Her entire brain focused on the movement. She squished her face against the locker wall and pulled the keys up. The easiest way to investigate the journal was to put the key-holder into her mouth. She had more room when she sat at a diagonal. With her thumb on the end of the small light, Sheridan opened the pages.

ALL MY HOPES AND DREAMS was written on the first sheet. Sheridan scanned the fat letters written with a rainbow of neon markers. If the doodled flowers with squiggled stems didn't prove a girl wrote the journal, the next line cinched it: *by Ribbon Barber.*

Chapter 4

Smart as a fifth grader. Ha Ha. I like that because I'm a fifth grader and I don't have to be any smarter than that.

Today I want to tell you about soup, so listen carefully.

Soup should be eaten with a fork. Not stew or chili. That's no big deal. I mean regular chicken noodle soup. It should have so many crackers crunched in that it won't slip through the poky part of a fork.

Now, if you've never done this before, be careful. There are good and bad ways to do it. If the soup is too hot then don't put all the crackers in at once or they get soggy. And your soup will just be gross. The crackers need to keep some of their crunch.

Also to the Dads out there trying to tell other fifth graders that dried croutons or thick bread does the same thing. Don't believe them. You want the crackers that are called "saltines." They're the best. For a full bowl of soup it can take an entire package to get the right thickness.

And always remember to save a few until the end. Just in case.

Chapter 5

Sheridan grinned. Finally, someone who knew the proper way to eat soup. She and Tex had argued over this concept at least a hundred times. This girl, Ribbon, knew the drill. The flowery drawings had worried Sheridan, who would have scribbled a knife on the page before she ever doodled a flower. But this kid was eclectic.

The world needed more people like Ribbon. The reason her locker was targeted became obvious. This girl was a threat to the status quo. Truly awesome people carry the biggest burden in high school. Even her name was neat. Her parents must be hippies or actors.

Sheridan let her thumb slip from the top of the penlight. In the darkness of the locker she tried to imagine what her new friend looked like. She probably had her natural eyebrows and some untamed hair around her face. That kind of beauty always made the predictable paper-doll cutouts nervous.

Wheels rattled on the tile floor.

Someone was in the hall.

The janitor.

"Hey!" She pounded on the locker door. "I'm in here. Number 572."

"¿Qué?"

"Hello. Please can you let me out?"

"What are you doing inside?" The man with the Spanish accent made the question sound like a statement. If he was the regular school janitor, he knew why she was inside. It probably wasn't his first rescue. "Por favor. You tell me the numbers for the combination?"

"Okay." Sheridan had to think. She'd only opened the locker a couple of times in her life and memorization wasn't a talent she possessed. "Is my backpack still there?"

"Si."

"There's a zipper at the top. The numbers are on the paper just inside." Her voice bounced off the walls. She probably didn't need to shout, but getting out of there and making it home would be good. She might just escape trouble with her new grown-ups. It wouldn't be good if they found out she'd gotten into it with some girls on the first day. Foster parents had suspicious natures. Kids were guilty until proven innocent.

After seven agonizing attempts, the locker door swung open, and Sheridan performed an awkward twist to free herself. The janitor wasn't shocked as Sheridan stretched stiff muscles. "Took you long enough."

The thirty-something man was about her same height. At four foot nine, she seldom had the chance to look a grown-up in the eye.

"I did not lock you in there." He gripped his mop and folded his arms across his chest.

"Of course not." Sheridan searched her bag to see if anything was missing.

"I don't steal."

"I never said you did." Sheridan shouldered her bag. She knew what it was like to be falsely accused. "I was checking to see if the idiots that locked me in took something."

"Okay." He relaxed.

"Thanks, Mr." She read the name embroidered on his uniform. "Talmadge."

"Por nada." He reached a small hand toward her. "My name's José. José Talmadge." The man's Mexican features matched his first name, but not his last. There was probably an interesting story connected to that. Sheridan liked stories and therefore liked this man.

"Sheridan. Sheridan Alexander."

"Nice to meet you."

"Thank you."

"School not always easy." He nodded at her. "Be careful."

"I will." She grabbed her boots from the locker hooks. His wet mop splattered onto the spilled V-8 juice. This school had its issues, and the Latino janitor with the English last name had probably seen the worst of it. Over a decade in the foster system had taught her to read ambivalence on the part of grown-ups. This man's eyes showed he cared. Of course, he had as little power to change things as she did. He might have the desire to stop the vandals but lacked the position.

With her boots zipped and her backpack slung over one shoulder, she stepped around Mr. Talmadge's wet floor. One thing those fake-hair, fashion slaves didn't understand was their games couldn't hurt Sheridan.

Even if all the other less-privileged kids in North Harbor High didn't have the guts to stand up to them, she would. Sheridan wanted to be more than a friend to Ribbon. She wanted to be an advocate. They'd rule these halls together.

Chapter 6

Today I found out I'm a weirdo.
That may sound stupid.
But how was I to know that other people cleaned their teeth with paste in a tube? We've always used baking soda. I asked Mom when I got home and she told me toothpaste wasn't earth friendly. And she should know. She's been teaching environmental science at the university forever. Dad too. Only he teaches geology.

Now I just have to figure out the other weird things we do to help Mother Earth. Mom says a lot of people don't care about the planet. I guess it wouldn't have been so bad if she told me about the toothpaste thing. Instead, I found out at Ashley's house. She's my best friend.

Here's what happened. Me and Ashley were walking home after the sixth-grade science fair. I tripped on a bumpy piece of sidewalk. Mostly because I couldn't see over my homemade model of Mars. I got a red ribbon. Anyway, the scrape on my knee didn't hurt too much, but there was lots of blood. When Ashley's mom saw it, she made me go inside so she could wash it.

Their whole house smelled like pumpkin pie. Even the bathroom smelled sweet. I couldn't believe it. Mrs. Nobel told me to sit on the side of the tub and put my leg on the closed toilet lid.

She used a soft wet rag to clean the top of my knee and squirted something on it that stung a little at first but then made the pain go away. In the drawer by the sink she pulled out a Band-

Aid, with that weird square, yellow cartoon character on it. One kid at school has the sponge guy on his backpack. Well, she left the drawer open and I saw a bright red tube.

When I asked her what it was she looked at me like I was from outer-space.

"Toothpaste. Don't you use toothpaste?"

I didn't say anything else because I didn't like the look on her face. When Mom came home from her afternoon class she told me all about toothpaste and how it contains pesticides and chemicals dangerous to bunnies and stuff.

All of this made sense except for one thing.

If this stuff was so bad, shouldn't somebody tell Mrs. Nobel about it?

Maybe another time. I'm not going back today so that she can look at me like I'm an alien or something.

Chapter 7

A shley left Courtney and the gang standing on the stairs after school. Why did Ribbon have to be such a pain? A little conformity never hurt anyone. It would have been better to leave it alone, but her old friend's absence bothered her. She dropped her backpack on the bed and ran out of the house before Dad could stop her. She searched her pocket. The envelope with one of the black-and-white prints was still there. The gift could be bartered for a conversation with Ribbon. Ashley double-checked the sidewalk behind her. Everyone knew where the Barbers lived. It was the favorite place for every disgusting Halloween prank.

Concrete squares patched a path from Ashley's house to their old hangout. She counted her steps with each chomp on her gum. As kids, Ashley and Ribbon spent most of their time on the swings now occupied by a couple of giggling ten-year-olds. Loves-me-loves-me-not daisy petals used to litter the way to a hollow bush where they shared all their elementary school secrets. Some of those were still in Ashley's vault. Nothing said to anyone. For what? She was risking her current high school status to go looking for someone who refused to stand up for herself. What a joke.

The park was the halfway point between where Ashley and Ribbon lived. The worn-grass path still led to the shortcut. It was a bit of a struggle to get through the hole in the fence. She'd grown in the last five years. The BFF she'd had in sixth grade was just too *different* for junior high. Ashley glanced over her shoulder one last time. Courtney must never find out. All hell would break loose. But what could Ashley do? Ribbon had pretty much vanished from school. For the first time since becoming friends with Courtney she was drawing outside of the leader's strict lines.

It was impossible to go back to junior high, but she couldn't help wishing for it. Not her entire eighth-grade year. But if she could, she would change the moment in the cafeteria when she decided to join up with Courtney. Dad would have eventually found a job. Instead, they were both slaves to Courtney and her father. And some of the blame goes to Ribbon. She better have a good explanation.

The Barber's house came into sight at the end of the street. Centered in the cul-de-sac, it remained a mystery. Ashley hadn't visited Ribbon in a long time. Not for a legitimate reason anyway. Even back in elementary, when they were friends, the Barbers weren't the sleepover kind of family. The brick structure wasn't a hangout.

In the front yard, the English garden grew wilder than Ashley remembered. Good. The plant invasion could hide her from the street. The front door stood like a wall before her. She scratched her forefinger with her thumbnail as she knocked.

A black-and-white cat batted the air after a bouncing moth. While its actions appeared playful, its intentions were deadly. The moth knew. That's why it flew higher. Why couldn't Ribbon do that? She should do something, anything. Shoot. If the girl decided to talk to her, Ashley would tell her, "Quit letting the gang get to you. It doesn't help."

Maybe Ribbon didn't ask for the harassment, but Ashley always wondered why she stayed for more. Why not fly above it?

Ashley studied the street one more time. Based on the overgrown weeds, the family might have moved. The porch stood in shadows. The sun shone on the other side of the house. The only way someone could see her would be with binoculars.

"What do you want?" Professor Barber's voice startled Ashley. She hadn't heard the door open. He stared at her from behind a half-closed door.

"Hi." Ashley brought her left ring finger to her mouth and began to nibble on the nail. Of course Ribbon would have told her parents about all the mean things going on at school. "I came by to see Ribbon."

"She's not here."

Ashley's heart pounded in her ears. She couldn't move as Ribbon's father glared at her. What was she doing? She rolled her gum around on her tongue. This was a bad idea.

"Ben." The soft word came from behind him. "Let me talk to her."

The screen swayed a little as Professor Barber turned and stomped away. A door slammed shut in the unseen depths of the house.

"Hi, Ashley." Mrs. Barber looked thin. She stepped out

onto the porch and closed the door behind her. "Sorry my husband's still a little upset."

"No problem. I should have called." The father of the nicest girl in the world was mad at her. She hadn't expected the rejection would turn her inside-out.

"Would you like to sit down?" Ribbon's mother pointed toward a couple wooden chairs on the porch.

"Sure." Ashley didn't search the street for spies. The wind pushed a breeze across the shaded porch. Courtney and the drama squad didn't matter for the moment. The smell of peppermint crossed her as Mrs. Barber passed. Ashley sat down. The sweet scent should have helped Ashley relax, but she couldn't help but think the Barbers knew all her sins. All the ugly words and mean actions. She fumbled into her pocket. It would take years to make it up to Ribbon. The photograph could be one day in the long journey. "I took this picture."

"Why would you take a picture of Ribbon?"

"I'm on the yearbook staff." It was the truth and a lie at the same time. Ashley's hand trembled as she passed the envelope to the woman. Ashley took the photos after school. Ribbon sat on a concrete bench in the churchyard alone. Not that Ribbon would be anything but alone. Ashley understood isolation, but Ribbon did it too much.

"Who told you about Ribbon?" Mrs. Barber fingered the envelope without opening the flap.

"Told me what?"

Silence held the breeze back. Ribbon's mother didn't answer. The dull look in her eyes scared the crackers out of Ashley. She shifted in her seat but couldn't shake the foreboding sensation floating around her. "Can I talk to her?"

"She's not here." Mrs. Barber squinted up at the clouds.

"When will she be back?" Ashley didn't want to push, but morbid thoughts began to rise in her mind. Ribbon was probably at her grandmother's. Yeah. Lots of kids moved away to find peace. The Barbers would do what they could to make Ribbon happy, even if they were a little weird. She shouldn't make too much out of this whole thing.

"Ribbon's not coming back." The sound of crinkled paper followed Mrs. Barber's words. The envelope rotated around the woman's fingers. She didn't open it. Over and over the enclosed photo of Ashley's old friend toppled in a mother's hands.

"I don't get it." Goosebumps prickled along Ashley's arms. She gripped the edge of her coat sleeves in her fist. Ashley couldn't remember if Mrs. Barber was always this quiet. The porch and house and setting might as well be new to Ashley. She'd knocked on the door before, but never spent more than a few minutes waiting for Ribbon to come play. Mostly they'd met up at the park. "Has she gone away to another school?"

"No." The older lady looked out at the neglected flowers in the yard. She cleared her throat and said, "Ribbon died."

Ashley's fingers went cold. She wrapped her arms around her body, still clinging tightly to the sleeves. "Of what?" Kids their age didn't die. Well, at least not kids like Ribbon. Right? She didn't have a car she would drive too fast. She didn't do drugs and stuff. How could Ribbon be dead?

Mrs. Barber answered with the calm of a news

reporter. "She killed herself."

Ashley couldn't move. The black-and-white photo crept into her mind. The direct gaze of sad eyes pierced her. The envelope in Mrs. Barber's hand probably contained the last recorded image of the ghost who would haunt Ashley for the rest of her life.

"We'd like to keep it private. Ribbon's life should be honored, not her death." Mrs. Barber stood. She gripped the doorpost, her knuckles white.

Ashley got up. What could she say? "I'm sorry. I didn't mean to cause any problems. It's just that I hadn't seen Ribbon around school and, well, we just hadn't hung out for so long I didn't know if she was okay or not." Ashley choked back any other words. She didn't have any right to be here, let alone cry.

Mrs. Barber went to the door. She didn't face Ashley when she said, "You were the best friend Ribbon ever had." The words burned like a slipped curling iron against Ashley's skin. Mrs. Barber went inside and closed the door without a bang.

Chapter 8

I hate junior high and I hate Ashley.

Everyone at school is mean to me just because I don't wear the same kind of clothes or cut my hair. And today Ashley just turned on me. I saved her a seat at lunch and when she walked by I called out to her. Stupid. Stupid. Stupid. I thought she didn't see me.

She did and so did everyone else.

They all started laughing when my former best friend sat with that stuck-up girl, Courtney. One kid started to make fun of me by mocking the way I called Ashley's name. Everyone laughed louder.

What's so funny about being mean? I don't know what I did wrong. Ashley and I used to do everything together. Now she pretends like she doesn't even know me.

I'm so confused and I feel stupid. The saddest thing of all. I know that if Ashley called me today and said she was sorry I'd totally forgive her.

How lame is that?

Chapter 9

"Sorry I'm so late," Sheridan repeated the lie she told Nina on the phone. "The research at the library took longer than I thought, then I missed the bus. It won't happen again, promise." Not the best way to start, but better than mentioning the locker incident. A janitorial rescue on the first day at school wouldn't make a good impression.

The grown-up's eyes brimmed with suspicion. "What's all over your hair?"

Oops, forgot about that. "Tomato juice." Sheridan had been so thrilled to escape she hadn't remembered. "V-8 to be exact. Some guy on the bus spilled it as he walked by."

"Hmm." Nina leaned against the kitchen counter. "Did you make any friends today?"

"Yeah, two." That wasn't a lie. Sheridan stuffed her hands in her pockets and crossed her fingers. She didn't want to explain that she counted as friends a girl in a journal and José Talmadge, the school's janitor.

"Good for you." Nina didn't ask. "Go get washed up.

Dinner starts in five minutes."

"You bet." She accepted the pass and hurried down the hall.

"Wait a minute."

Sheridan skidded to a stop. Even from across the room Nina's stance was crammed full of expectation. "You spent money today, right?"

"Yes."

"Okay, for what?"

"Lunch and bus fare."

"Log it on the chart. Every penny. It's best to make that a habit as soon as you walk in the door."

Sheridan nodded and smiled without meaning it.

"Just think, by the end of the week you'll have a bus pass from the school. That will be a good way to save."

"Absolutely."

Ribbon's journal would have to wait. The best thing about new foster folks was the honeymoon period. The days when they pretended to love you like their own. Sheridan pretended too. That's what happened when strangers came together and were forced to be families. Everyone smiled, all hopeful and shiny like a new penny. But Sheridan knew copper turned puke green over time.

She entered Nina's budget-room. One dry-erase board was lined with black plastic tape. It was a refillable calendar. Sheridan picked up the blue marker Nina had assigned to her and wrote in her daily expenses. Other boards contained pie charts and graphs Sheridan would be forced to understand later.

Nina wasn't going to let too much slide. Sheridan's decision to not fight back at school today had been a good one. This grown-up had no chart for trouble. So

Sheridan played the happy-kid through dinner, finished her homework and chores, then excused herself.

Safe in her room, she plopped down on the striped comforter and thought about Ribbon. Besides soup and crackers, the girl also liked the color red and the smell of freshly mowed grass. The similarities didn't end there. They were both born in February. Sheridan had the misfortune of being born the day after Valentine's Day. She missed being loved by a few hours. With Ribbon being born on February 10, the world was full of hearts and hugs and kisses when the girl was four days old. Her doodled flowers made sense.

Sheridan pushed herself up from the bed. The floorboards in the hall creaked under her feet. Nina and Joe watched TV in the living room. Sheridan tiptoed into the kitchen. It wasn't like she searched the cupboards for alcohol or cigarettes. Still, the tension buzzed through her. Noise might rat her out. The odds of home number six being worse than this were extremely high.

The orange box sat in the skinny cupboard next to the stove. She scooped a spoonful of the baking soda onto a small plate. Nina and Joe laughed at their program, and Sheridan hurried back down the hall.

It wasn't necessary, but she locked the bathroom door anyway. The journal and locker and Ribbon were her secret for now. She didn't want a repeat of the farm where adults had told her to ignore what she felt. Not this time.

Ribbon's home life was odd. While her parents weren't hippies or actors, they were strange. Baking soda to brush your teeth. Gross. Sheridan knew foster homes could be strange places. But apparently so could regular families. In one entry, Ribbon explained how she used a safety pin to release the ingrown hairs from her unshaved legs. The Barbers only allowed one gallon of water each day to bathe with. Crazy.

In her first attempt to use the baking soda, the powder didn't stick to the dry toothbrush. She turned on the water and wet the bristles. The white grains grabbed the water in globs, but not enough to clean her teeth. She tried it again with her brush really wet. As the water dripped from the green plastic spikes, the soda absorbed it like a hungry bird. Sheridan put the plate under the dripping faucet. The particles mixed with water to make a paste. Interesting. Kind of like a third-grade science project, only different.

With enough goop on the end of her brush, she took a deep breath and stared at herself in the mirror. "There is no way this is going to taste minty," she said aloud, "but here goes."

The first taste wasn't bad. Very salty.

Sheridan continued until she reached the inside of her back teeth. The baking soda touched her tongue a few too many times. Her face twisted into a squint and she spat out the homemade concoction.

It wasn't bitter, but the salty taste and grainy texture were disgusting. She wouldn't want the Barbers to be her foster parents. It took a gallon of water to rinse her mouth free of the stuff. Her teeth were clean—she had to admit that. But what a joke.

Sheridan had to find this girl, if only to let her try toothpaste. She sent a text message to Tex. If anyone could find the previous owner of locker 572 it would be her favorite foster brother. She couldn't fix the system. For her, family meant stress and strangers. Those who didn't prey on the weak ignored them or closed their eyes. The pervert at the farm never touched her. She sometimes wished he would have tried it. She would have broken more than his nose. Sheridan wanted to blame the wife but couldn't. That blind incrimination would come too close to her and Tex as well.

The obvious wasn't always obvious.

Chapter 10

A shley didn't look for high school spies on her walk home. She didn't look for daisy petals either. When the rough edge of the fence tore a hole in Ashley's shirt, she didn't care. Ribbon was dead. Stupid girl. STUPID, STUPID, STUPID.

Her lungs tightened as she moved through the shortcut in a daze. Children laughed on the swings and clouds shifted in the sky. And Ashley's feet moved one in front of the other. No one she knew ever died before. People in her life didn't stop thinking or talking or breathing.

The sun shone harsh and angry. Stupid kids laughed and played as if there wasn't a junior high or high school in their future. Great. Most of them actually looked forward to it. If she could shake one of them she would. Don't make friends with people. Don't do it. Ribbon, what a selfish, selfish, selfish thing to do.

Oh man. Ashley blinked hard then swallowed her anger. This wasn't happening. It couldn't be. Each step took her closer to home and further from hope. A block from her house, the sound of her cell phone startled her. Courtney. Great. The last person on earth Ashley wanted to talk to right now. The continuous ring of a party song from the phone grated against her nerves.

"Hello."

"Hey, Ashley, what's up?"

"Nothing." It was pointless to tell her anything about Ribbon.

"Cool." The relaxed tone of Courtney's voice sounded ridiculous in Ashley's brain. "Have you finished our chemistry homework yet?"

"I'm not home."

"I thought you were grounded."

"Yeah." Ashley stopped and tapped her foot on the sidewalk. Five minutes ago, caring about Courtney's endless demands evaporated with Ribbon's spirit. So did homework and haters.

"Where'd you go?"

"Nowhere." What if Ashley just said it? Ribbon's dead, you control freak. Are you happy now? Forget about it. Might as well ask what would happen if the earth split in two.

"What's wrong with you?"

"I'm just tired, is that okay with you?"

"Hey, don't bite my head off."

Ashley didn't answer. Courtney never tolerated anyone else's bad moods. This so-called friend threatened everyone with her father's big job and school board position. More than a couple of kids were expelled from school or sent to detention on the word of Courtney alone. Well, not really alone. She always had some troll to support her.

"Hello. Are you still there?" Ashley pictured

Courtney's hand on her hip. So what. Ashley was over it. Over Ribbon. Over Courtney. Over every freaking thing in life.

"I asked when the chemistry homework would be done."

Ashley didn't answer. Breaking down the molecules of soda pop held zero importance to her. Let Courtney do her own homework for a change.

"Hello. Are you still there?"

"Look, I've got to go. I'll talk to you later." Ashley's fingers tingled with adrenaline as she pushed the off button. She had never spoken to Courtney like that, let alone hung up on her. All the seemingly important things from yesterday had blown away with Ribbon's daisy petals. Ashley couldn't take away all the mean things she said and did to Ribbon, but maybe she could stop feeding the monster.

The swing on Ashley's front porch rocked back and forth. She sat and let it sway on its own. The impossibility of Ribbon's death weighed on her shoulders and neck. Her former friend killed herself. Gave up on life. What would it have been like to have been Ribbon? No friends. In fact, the only person who was ever nice to her joined the haters in junior high.

A roly-poly crawled across the wooden porch. Its tiny legs moved over the concrete in no clear direction. It wandered and bumped into a small twig and blindly bounced its way around the obstacle until it was free. Ashley resisted the temptation to tap it with the tip of her shoe to make it curl up into the tight ball.

You were the best friend Ribbon ever had. Mrs. Barber's words climbed with piercing claws all over Ashley's nerves. The sad thing. It was true. Nobody liked Ribbon.

If they did, they didn't dare tell anyone. High school science taught survival of the fittest. Kill or be killed. But Ribbon was supposed to fight back, not flee. Never suicide. What would Darwin say about that?

The roly-poly made its way around the post toward the stairs. Somehow the rotation of the earth should have hiccupped. A real, live person was dead. And Ashley was part of the swarm who stung her daily. This wasn't a small thing.

The phone in her hand vibrated with a new text message. She didn't have to look to know it was from Courtney.

Chapter 11

Eighth grade graduation was a week ago. Today I sat in the window of my room and imagined skipping around the tree in my neighbor's backyard. A big palm grew, surrounded by thick grass, unhampered by a vegetable garden. Sometimes I dream while I'm awake. As I watch myself circle the tree, one hand felt the rough uneven slats against my fingertips. My chin and neck were exposed to open sky. I lifted my voice and sang.

"Sticks and stones will break my bones, but words will never hurt me."

I like that me. The one that swirled in a plaid skirt.

"Sticks and stones."

A red sock slipped down to my blue shoes. I bent to pull it back up to my knee.

"Will break my bones."

I skipped again. My crisp white shirt came untucked from my waist.

"But words will never hurt me."

The image blurred. Rain covered the window winning its battle over the sun that still shown from an unseen corner of the sky.

Chapter 12

Sheridan slapped the journal closed. People are vicious. In fact, all the horrible, awful, tangled mess that made up injustice tore at her. From the open door to her room, the smell of chocolate chips assaulted her. The homey fragrance didn't mix well in her stomach. It was Elsie all over again. Where was her little foster sister from the farm now?

"Hey there." Nina poked her head into the room.

Sheridan forced a smile to her face.

"*Survivor* starts in about fifteen minutes." Nina was determined to play Mom. "I made treats."

"I can't wait." Sheridan held back the frustrated scream which wrestled in her throat.

Nina left, wiping her hands on her apron.

Sheridan slid Ribbon's journal into the desk drawer and walked into the bathroom to splash water on her face. Maybe she should write to the producers of Nina's favorite reality show. They could send the next group of castaways into the wilderness called "high school." Let's see how long they could survive in that jungle.

Chapter 13

A shley kept her bedroom door ajar. According to her father's favorite weatherman, it was sunny and warm in San Diego. Ribbon's ghost stared at Ashley through the water spots on the photo. Of the seven pictures taken, this was the last one Ashley shot before putting her camera down that day. Did Ribbon see her? She'd followed her old friend from school to the church, parked across the street, and held the camera through her car window. Her former friend had looked directly into the camera. In the photo, a haunting look of resolve dulled the girl's eyes.

The late local news broadcasted the state of the world. Ashley heard the television from her bedroom. She paid enough attention to the reports to know life sucked. Violence and hatred and death ruled the world. Fox News might only shout about it at 6:00 P.M. and 10:00 P.M., but it was the truth around the clock.

Mom kicked Dad out when Ashley was in sixth grade. In junior high, Courtney's father gave Dad a job. By the time he got clean and sober, it was too late. Mom

had a new boyfriend. Ashley moved back with her Dad
when Mom's new husband found work in Arizona. Mom
hadn't fought for custody. That didn't matter. Ashley
wanted to stay in the same neighborhood and not
disrupt her social life by a big move in the middle of her
adolescence. Would it have been better to start over in
Phoenix? Hard to say now.

When the voices from the television stopped, the
floorboards creaked, and Dad headed to bed. Ashley
refreshed her gum. Water gurgled through the pipes.
Ashley pushed herself away from her desk and grabbed
her coat. She couldn't sleep. The shower in Dad's
bathroom would block the click of the deadbolt and the
distant start of her car at the curb. Ashley needed to go
for a drive. Maybe visit the last place she'd seen Ribbon.
She had to confirm whether or not Ribbon saw her from
that bench. Her former friend might have decided to do
it that day. If she had noticed Ashley in the car outside
the church taking her picture, it could have pushed the
girl over the edge.

Ashley fought back tears and worked on her gum.
The streets were empty this late on a Wednesday night.
Ashley parked on the same side of the street she had two
weeks ago. Thanks to a lamppost, the bench Ribbon used
was highlighted. If Ashley had any guts, she would take a
picture of the deserted bench in the churchyard and print
the two photos side by side in the yearbook as a
memorial. Not a bad idea, except she didn't bring her
camera.

The church parking lot was as unpopulated as any
cemetery. Ashley left her car on the street and headed for
the bench. A cool breeze pricked her cheeks. The sound
of another car door slamming down the road made her

jump. Ashley wasn't the type to chase the dead, and the idea of Ribbon being gone caused bumps to prickle up her arm.

The dark suburb was safe. Right? The only person who might approach her would be some dweeb taking out the trash. She really didn't want to deal with anyone, good or bad. If an over-protective adult did ask what she was doing out so late, she'd find a lame excuse. Maybe she'd tell them she was praying. People prayed at churches. Right?

No one stopped her. At the bench, the light broke up the shadows. Ashley sat down. The cold concrete drew shivers to her bottom. It would have been warmer when Ribbon was here. Ashley looked toward the car. She couldn't see anything beyond the circle of lamplight. The obvious problem presented itself. The view would be different at night. Ribbon had sat here during the daytime. The neighborhood would have been visible during the day. She'd have to come back tomorrow with her camera.

Regardless of what Ribbon might have thought, Ashley never planned to do anything mean with the pictures. But Ribbon wouldn't know that. The girl would have every right to think the prints would be decapitated and reattached in the print shop in some Frankenstein way. Courtney would have plastered them around the school with some vulgar saying on them. That wasn't the goal. The gang might have changed Ashley's original reason. Survival of the fittest. Of course, that wouldn't be necessary now. None of the kids from school knew about the pictures. In fact, they didn't even miss Ribbon. They'd turned their attention to the new girl, Tinkerbell.

A twig cracked behind her and she whipped her head around. The gate on the opposite side of the church was swallowed in darkness. She heard a giggle to her left and started to get up when Courtney plopped down on the bench to her right.

"Whatcha doing?"

"Oh crackers!" Ashley sank back down onto the bench. "You scared me."

"Did I?" Leaves quivered on the tree above the light post to Ashley's left. Ten other girls surrounded the bench. Helen was the first to speak.

"Maybe she's doing her chemistry homework."

The other girls laughed.

Ashley took a deep breath and studied the ground.

It wasn't coincidence that brought them all together. Ashley knew the script. Courtney had assigned a couple of low-on-the-food-chain girls to watch her twenty-four hours a day. A group text message would have done the rest. The princess had to remind the group she ruled this kingdom. It would have happened today or next week or eventually. Who cares? Ribbon's dead. Ashley looked straight ahead. None of them were as guilty as she was. Ribbon had been her friend, not theirs. Let them beat her up. It didn't matter.

The gang didn't move. The best way to get it over with was to try to leave. Ashley stood. She'd been here before. Not in this position, but here, next to Courtney, when she reined in a situation that got out of hand. It was Ashley's turn to submit.

"So, what happened today?" Courtney stood.

"I just had a bad day." The glow around the bench ended in two steps. Ashley took the first one.

"And that gives you a right to take it out on me?"

Courtney matched the step.

"No." Ashley's second step carried her into the darkness. The first slap burned across her cheek. Ashley didn't turn back toward the attacker. This wasn't a time to be proud. She flinched as a smack stung the back of her head. Strong hands pushed her into another person.

Before she could block the next blow, one of her friends grabbed her shoulders and pulled their knee hard against her ribs. Ashley folded in half. She tried to catch her breath while a storm of fists pelted her on every side. The sharp pain from every angle couldn't be shielded. She rolled onto the ground and curled up.

Instinct pulled her hands over her head. It was all she could do. The least amount of damage to her face the better. Feet kicked and stomped on her legs and arms. Hands and fists smacked hard against her head. The beat-fest lasted probably less than a minute before Courtney told them to stop.

"Eat dirt, you slimy whore." Ashley recognized Helen's voice and heard her hock a loogie. The snot-covered spitball slid down Ashley's uncovered neck.

"That's enough."

Feet shuffled backward. The sound of heavy breathing mixed with the breeze. Ashley flinched as someone touched her on the back and leaned close to her face. Courtney's calm voice came close to her ear. "Sorry we had to do this. It's only a warning. To get back on my good side, show me what you can do to the new girl."

Ashley didn't answer.

"It would be horrible if my father had to find out about this." Courtney's whisper echoed through Ashley's brain.

The cool lawn held her body as the laughter and

insults faded from the churchyard. The smell of grass and dirt pulled at a strange memory—the only time Ashley had seen Courtney vulnerable. The summer between eighth and ninth grade a group of kids got together to play a combination of tag and hide-and-go-seek. Ashley had found a spot next to a fence where the grass sloped. She pressed her face against the grass and waited for the "ollie ollie oxen free" call.

When she got back to the group, it was already disbanding. The slow summer sun had finally dropped low enough to cause the streetlight to flicker on. The universal signal had kids heading home. Ashley walked over to Courtney's yard and grabbed her bike. It was a mile or so home, and Dad always freaked out when it got dark.

Courtney sat on the curb.

"Aren't you going inside?"

"No." Courtney pushed a stick into the gap between the concrete gutter and the tar road. "I don't have a curfew."

"Wow, you're lucky." Ashley spun the pedals of her ten-speed before planting her weight on one to balance.

"My folks don't care when I come home."

Ashley thought that would be sad as she pedaled home. Since Mom left, Dad cared to the point of obsession. But what would it be like if he didn't care at all?

Chapter 14

Sheridan was up by six-o'clock in the morning. Three years on the farm had trained her. Other kids might hit the snooze and dread the day, but not her. She refused to start her day limp. It worked out good in this house. Joe would drive her to school instead of her having to take the city bus. Another "win" for Nina's save chart.

With her teeth clean, the new North Harbor High senior dropped her toothbrush into the glass by the sink and checked her face for pimples. Before she could discover anything, Nina stepped into the doorframe.

"Do you know what time it is?" Nina's hair was tussled and sleep still weighed on her eyelids. "Six-thirty." She extended the cordless phone in Sheridan's direction. "Too early for people to be calling." The grown-up raised two tired eyebrows. "Especially a boy."

"Right." Probably Tex. Why would he call the house instead of her cell?

"Tell him no calls before school."

"Absolutely." Sheridan kept her hand over the

receiver until she entered her room. "What the heck are you doing?"

"I tried yer cell phone three times." Tex's fake drawl was agitated.

"I was in the bathroom."

"Makes no never mind. Lookie here. Ya need ta be careful at that school."

"No duh!"

"Seriously, the kids there are more dangerous than a stallion on steroids."

"Did you think I was exaggerating about the locker?"

"That's nothing."

"Nothing? You try folding your lanky butt into a metal box."

"Are ya on yer computer?" Tex sounded impatient. He wasn't usually like that.

"I told you I just got out of the bathroom."

"Well, now that yer out, mind moseying over to your machine?"

"Fine." Sheridan went to the desk and followed Tex's instructions to a website.

"Now, these rascals archive their chat logs every couple a days or so. But I found a way to hack into old conversations."

Sheridan scrolled down. "Whew!" The words polluting the site were worse than those scratched into locker 572. Her soul ached. Ribbon needed more help than ever. She scrolled to the last date where Tex had found Ribbon's name.

> **Princess17:** ring around the toilet, you are a loser. Jeremy never liked you. it was all a joke and you were the punch line, you're so weak, what makes

you think that anyone would want to study with a hacked up face like yours? only plastic surgery can help you. go slit yourself no guy will ever want you. forget that, no girl would want you. you're life is a waste.
Sept 28 at 10:02 P.M.

12 people *like* this.

RibbonB: Fine. I'll go ahead and kill myself to make you happy.
Sept 28 at 10:25 P.M.

Hottie-girl: Ribbon... what's the b stand for? (lol) go wet yourself
Sept 28 at 10:26 P.M.

got2begood: you always say you'll kill yourself. Waaaa. you big baby. lame, you're not bad enough to do it. piece of garbage.
Sept 28 at 10:28 P.M.

Princess17: i say hurry up and die, you skank. Do it yourself before we do it for you.
Sept 28 at 10:30 P.M.

"This is messed up," Sheridan complained into the receiver. The messaging continued with f-bombs and at least four more death threats. Sheridan pushed herself away from the computer. How could people do this? Her stomach felt queasy reading it.

"And this ain't the R-rated stuff," Tex said.

"Did you find out where Ribbon went?"

"No. Her folks teach at the university." Tex gave Sheridan the address and phone number of the Barbers.

"Look. Ya need ta be careful. There's no telling what them kids are capable of. And I live too far away ta help."

The thought made Sheridan want to laugh. Tex might be taller than her but he weighed the same. She could out-fight him on her worse day.

"Listen, hero, you've got to help me find out the names behind 'got2begood,' 'Hottie-girl,' and 'princess17.' RibbonB must be for Ribbon, but why would they call her 'ring around the toilet'?"

"I'm not some puppy ya get to boss around."

"Whatever."

"Besides, I already did it. The central characters on the site are Helen Robinson, Courtney Manchester, and Ashley Nobel. Although, the Ashley gal hasn't been as active since July."

"There's an Ashley in Ribbon's journal."

"It's a common name."

"Maybe. Can you help me get onto the site without being tracked?"

"Can I go to school first?"

"I guess. But Tex, I'm worried about this Ribbon girl."

"Yeah, me too. I'll text ya some untraceable log-on names. That'll give ya a chance to fight undercover."

"Perfect." Sheridan hung up and shut down the computer. From the open door to her room, the smell of coffee floated down the hall. She studied the shoes in her closet and decided on a pair of red ballet flats. Never knew what adventure awaited her at North Harbor. As Nina and Joe drank jolts of caffeine, Sheridan opened Ribbon's journal. There had to be more clues.

Chapter 15

This is the worst day of my life.

I forgot to flush the toilet at school, and the meanest girl at North Harbor High used the stall right after me. Then to make matters worse, she ran around the school telling everyone I peed my pants. That's a total lie. I thought it would be better once I got out of junior high. Fat chance. High school's worse. Why *do* I have to be the only kid in the world with parents who are environmental nutcases?

Dad says there's nothing wrong with waiting to flush until you have a bowel movement. Well, Dad, tell that to Courtney Manchester and every other earth-hating jerk at school. Tell them all about water conservation if you can. I tried but they only laughed.

Mom's no better. She told me our toilets are cleaner than anyone else in the neighborhood. I guess most people only clean their bathrooms once per week. But we put in baking soda and scrub it every time we flush. She says I should be proud of myself for standing up for the next generation.

Right. Proud of people calling me "Ring around the toilet." Yeah, that's my new nickname, you like it? Saving water doesn't make up for the kids who throw things at me during lunch or torment me online. I'm definitely not going to school tomorrow. I just can't.

I even tried to talk to my counselor, Miss

Jones. She wanted names and places and promised to contact their parents. As if that would make it better. That doesn't work. Every seventh grader in the world knows that, and I'm a freshman in high school. She went with the fallback propaganda —"they're jealous."

Is the entire adult population blind? These rich, beautiful, popular kids are NOT jealous of me. I'm so ready to get out of here I could die. I'd like to move away from home and live a normal life. I'm just afraid I won't survive my freshman year.

I feel so alone. The only friend I've ever had hates my guts and I have NO clue why. I don't understand. She hits me in the hall and calls me horrible names. Everyone swears at me. It hurts so bad the only thing I think that will ever make it go away is death. But thinking of that makes me a disgusting person.

Chapter 16

F unny thing about thoughts, if they wander too far away from home they get lost. Ashley couldn't be like Mary and her little lamb, waiting for them to come home. She locked the darkroom door and flipped on the outside light. Courtney's demands had to be followed. Ashley couldn't care less about her social life anymore, but Dad worked for Mr. Manchester and that bridge was too dangerous to destroy.

Ribbon was gone and nothing would change that. Ashley had a choice between protecting Tinkerbell or her dad. The new girl meant nothing to her. It was a no-brainer. The new girl was going down. Life was hard.

Ashley flattened her chewed Trident against her teeth then made small popping sounds with it. With two years left in this hole, the next dozen months required putting up with both Courtney's *and* Helen's demands. At least until something else came up for Ashley and her dad.

The fifth period math class she shared with Tinkerbell started in five minutes. In the masked solitude of the darkroom, she opened the bottle of blushing berry fingernail polish and poured it in globs over the absorbent cotton of a Maxi pad.

What did she care about the new girl? Ashley had a right to survive. Maybe she could sign up for work-study next year. She leaned against the counter and pressed her hand on her troubled stomach. The bruises on her legs and arms ached.

The group had never jumped Ribbon. They wouldn't risk it. Courtney preferred harder-to-trace verbal assaults. For more than one week last year, everyone got a point for each time they smacked Ribbon in the back of the head. Those kinds of attacks never provided enough evidence to get anyone suspended.

Ribbon didn't complain. It was pointless. Courtney never got in trouble. The girl was Teflon. Ashley had no idea how Mr. Manchester made his millions. But she knew his position with the school board worked well for Courtney. Ashley had seen a ton of kids get kicked out of school because of the queen bee. Some were even in juvie.

The bell sounded the one-minute warning for class to start. Ashley scooped up the painted pad and put it in a paper bag. She held the sack in her hand like a third grader's lunch and left the darkroom.

In the classroom, she found a seat in the back corner. The first forty-nine minutes might as well have been forty-nine hours. Ashley must have wiped the sweat from her palms a hundred times. She had to time this just right for it to work. There was a chance it would flop. But if it worked, she'd be back in Courtney's graces. In fact, her so-called friend would love the new spin on the old trick they played in junior high. Pat a kid on the back while you taped on a piece of paper that said "Kick me, I'm a dork."

When the clock indicated one minute to the bell, Ashley got ready. With her hands under her desk, she opened the bag and slipped out the stained napkin. The bag crinkled. She slowed down. No one looked in her direction. Good.

Forty-five seconds left. She peeled back the tabs to the adhesive and tucked them into her back pocket. With the pad still hidden, she reached into her other pocket and took out the five-dollar bill she'd saved for this moment.

Thirty seconds. She had to lay the pad in her lap in order to put away her notebook. The girl next to her gasped. Ashley pressed her index finger against her lips then burned a glare into the girl, until the dweeb remembered to mind her own business.

Fifteen seconds. Other kids had been watching the clock, and the noise of chairs against tile masked the sound made when Ashley folded the empty paper sack and put it in her textbook.

The clock in the corner ticked away the remaining seconds before the bell. The second hand jerked from fifty-eight to fifty-nine to the top of the hour. The speakers chimed three times, and the noise level in the class exploded.

Tinkerbell pulled her backpack out from under her desk at the front of the room. With all of her stuff ready, Ashley joined the throng of students at the door, slipping behind her victim. She was about to tag the girl when she noticed the teacher watching. It would be better to get her in the hall. She only hoped the adhesive wouldn't stop working.

In the wider traffic of the hallway, Ashley palmed the red-painted section of the pad and pressed her hand against Sheridan's lower back, just below her backpack. "Hey."

"What?" The new girl took on a defensive pose.

"This was on the floor by your desk." Ashley held out the five-dollar bill toward her victim. "I wondered if you dropped it."

"I don't think so." Sheridan patted her pockets.

"Whatever." Ashley crinkled the bill into her fist then made a loud pop with her gum before she walked away.

Chapter 17

Sheridan preferred stomping to skipping. But a couple of times through the day she fought back the urge to do a happy cartwheel. The anticipation at meeting Ribbon had bubbled in her like a 7-Up commercial. By the last class however, the twits at school turned her good mood warm and flat.

Laughter attacked her through the halls.

The finger pointing made it obvious the joke was on her.

Usually, high school hallways have history, but the people around her were total strangers. In a couple of days, Sheridan had become an outcast. As a foster child she never struggled to find someone to hang out with. Grown-ups had always been her enemy. Now, the whole school seemed pitted against her.

She entered French class and looked forward to getting to the library so she could strike back—anonymously of course. Graduation was still important to her. More than important. It meant freedom from the clutches of the state of California. In half a dozen months she'd never have to *"Parlez vous"* with these people again. And today she had an appointment with an Internet site. She'd say plenty then.

"Pardonne moi." Her teacher pulled her aside as if it were a secret. "You've got something stuck to your *derrière."*

Sheridan reached back and removed the disgusting joke.

The entire class exploded in laughter. One boy swooned and went pale. Sheridan pretended to throw it at him, and he screamed like a second-grade girl. The idiots turned on him. The only person who did absolutely nothing was the teacher. Sheridan glared at the woman, who became very interested in the notes on her desk.

The disgusting pad landed in the trash can with a thud. A stupid prank like that would crush someone with a tender nature like Ribbon. But these punks were messing with the wrong girl. Shoot. If a lifetime in foster care didn't harden you, what did? Sheridan wanted to shout, "Bring it."

She dusted her hands and headed to her desk more angry than embarrassed. They wouldn't know what hit them. Good thing Tex was ten steps ahead of them. In her seat she pulled out her cell phone. "I found one of them. Or I should say..." Sheridan struggled to find the letters on her keypad. She'd never had a phone of her own, and she couldn't text as fast as most kids her age. The cryptic codes were not part of her vocabulary. "...she found me." Sheridan clicked send.

"What happened?" Tex replied before the bell for class rang.

Sheridan typed, "Too juvenile to spell out. Class is

starting. Later."

Her phone vibrated Tex's single letter "k" response.

She forced herself to conjugate verbs. She was more hacked off at the teacher than she was the stupid kids. The imbecile at the front of the room started class without one word about the bad joke, or even saying a word to the hecklers. Sheridan pushed her irregular French verbs to the side and pulled out Ribbon's journal.

Adults were cowards. Not one of them had the strength, let alone the desire, to do what was necessary to control the rich bullies. Time to tell those fakers the game was on. Maybe every other underprivileged kid in North Harbor High could be controlled by them. But not Sheridan. And now, not Ribbon. Wherever the girl was, she had a friend in Sheridan.

Chapter 18

It's a horrible habit, like smoking. I know it's killing me but I just can't stop going to see what they write about me on the Internet. I no longer try to defend myself. It only makes things worse. I just cover myself in a thick haze and decide they are probably right.

I know I never wet myself, but the other stuff seems true.

The words just follow me around like a cloud. Stupidity creeps up on me. Ugly and worthless cover me. I don't want to be that way, but what else can I think? If everyone in the world agrees, then it must be true.

To be honest, my parents are wackos. Really. Who lives in the city and grows their own food and makes their own soap and recycles every single solitary thing? Mom makes paper out of dryer lint. For crying out loud, we don't even have a clothes dryer. She goes door to door to collect lint from neighbors.

Mom, your homemade plaques don't mean anything. Neither do the expressions from a bunch of dead people. Who cares that Eleanor Roosevelt said, "Great minds discuss ideas, average minds discuss events, small minds discuss people?" Blah, blah, blah, blah. Maybe that was true a million years ago. But NOT NOW!

Chapter 19

"No more nicey-nice, Tex." Sheridan lowered her voice as she entered the library. "Let's squash those cyber creeps."

"You betcha."

"We need to let Ribbon know she's not alone." An old man glared at her from the computer next to her and then pointed to the no-cell-phone sign. "I can't talk in here."

"I'll do the talking. Do ya have something ta write with?"

"Just a minute." She grabbed a scrap of paper. The miniature pencil fumbled in her fingers a couple of times before she got a good grasp. She preferred to think it was adrenaline and not nerves causing her to struggle with the small writing tool.

"Okay. Ready."

"Log onto the site with this sign-on. V-E-N-G-E-A-N-C-E-1."

"Nice."

"So untraceable not even the CIA could find ya." Tex was a genius. No one was better at this stuff than him.

"Besides, the queen bee doesn't like visitors."

"Who?"

"The archives show this gal, Courtney, yanks access from the people who ruffle her feathers. Her log-on name is Princess17. Keep a keen eye on her, she's vicious."

"Can't she make the site private?"

"Then it wouldn't be *public* humiliation."

"Good point." The old man stood up, and Sheridan hurried back to the library entrance. "I've got to hang up. No phones in the computer area, and there's an old guy ready to play rent-a-cop."

"'kay. Just be ready, this group'll cut ya off quick. When they do, sign-on again as 'vengeance2' and so on. I made 10 of 'em to play with."

"Why?" Sheridan put the paper on the library wall and wrote down the password for each sign-on.

"You'll see. Just be careful."

"I'm not scared of these idiots." Sheridan stepped aside for a mother and her daughter to exit with a handful of picture books.

"We still don't know what happened ta Ribbon." Tex's drawl was heavy.

"Do you think they really hurt her? I mean, physically?"

"All I know is the gal ain't on any school register in San Diego County."

"Maybe they moved." Sheridan kicked her red ballet flat against the wall. This sucked. To think some of these kids were a couple years or a handful of months away from becoming voters was messed up. Ribbon shouldn't have to go in hiding.

"Her folks still work at the university." Tex took a deep breath. "Look, Sis, nobody just disappears."

"She could be hiding out." She said it more like a prayer than a thought.

"That'd be nice. But she's completely off the grid. These varmints could be dangerous."

"I'd like to see them try to do something to me."

"Whoa, slow down. Keep yer guns in yer holster. Stay low. Got it?"

"I don't know." The thought of a dead Ribbon in Sheridan's mind wasn't new. But Tex made it sound more possible. Two people with the same thought increased the likeliness of it being true. Especially since Ribbon had left the school without her journal. Kids didn't abandon thoughts this private.

Chapter 20

I hate them. Every one of them.

I hate my mother and my father and all their stupid rules.

I hate Ashley and every stupid girl at school.

I still can't believe what happened in the showers at school. They made me strip naked. No underwear. No towel. Nothing. Just my horrible ugly body shoved under the cold water. Six girls, Ashley included, squirted liquid soap and shampoo at me while they laughed. When I curled up in the corner they didn't stop.

I bathe! EVERY DAY, I BATHE. Not at school. Never at school. Showers are against Dad's water conservation rules.

What am I going to do?

It took more than the gallon I'm allowed each day to get the toothpaste out of my hair. That's all I need. If Dad finds out, he'll explode.

I can't take it anymore.

It's not worth it.

None of it.

Chapter 21

Ashley threw a towel over her shoulder and headed past the gym lockers to the showers. Three girls bumped past her in a hurry. That's not good. She would have turned around if Maddie hadn't waved her over.

The thinnest member of the gang pushed open the door to the shower room. She was the watch dog. Just like last month with Ribbon. Was it Ashley's turn?

"Hey, Maddie."

"Hi, Ash. Great joke today on the new girl."

"Thanks." Ashley gritted her teeth. Maybe it wasn't a planned hazing after all.

Inside the moist room, Courtney, Helen, and three other followers waited for Ashley. They stopped talking when they saw her. Ashley didn't wipe the sweat from her hands. She grabbed the towel around her neck with her fists and yanked down. "What's up?"

"Good job today." Courtney was here to pee on her tree and secure her territory.

"You still grounded?" Helen leaned back on the tile wall.

"Nope." Ashley kept her eyes on Courtney.

The leader tossed a bottle of liquid soap to Helen. "Give that to Ashley."

Helen smugly obeyed.

"Hurry up and get clean." Courtney came close to Ashley without touching her. "Because we're going to the Web today. And I expect to see you signed on. No more disappearing acts."

"I thought I proved that to you today." Ashley fought to keep her tone even.

"You did." Courtney laughed. "I just wanted to make sure. Come on girls, let's give Ashley some privacy."

Her so-called pals left her in the wet room. She sat down on the wooden bench and watched the walls sweat. High school sucked. And she was part of the reason. It was no coincidence Courtney had brought her into the place where they delivered Ribbon's ultimate humiliation.

That day scalded Ashley's heart like no other. Courtney had become addicted to abusing Ribbon. The leader needed more and more violence to feed her fix. Ashley threw her towel on the floor. If she was honest with herself, it was why she started to follow Ribbon. Maybe even why she took the girl's picture. The group had become too mean and over the top.

They didn't hit Ribbon. They didn't touch her. Not her body anyway.

Instead, they tortured her soul. Every day, Ashley waited to get called into the counselor's office, but Ribbon must have locked it into her heart. No one spoke of it again. Ribbon stopped going to the gym. In fact, she quit everything.

Ashley suddenly felt dirty. She kept her clothes on while she wet her hair. In the bathroom, she removed her contacts and cleaned off the make-up from her face. In a faded sweatshirt and her old glasses, she headed to the library.

Chapter 22

Sheridan tried not to scream into the phone. "I'm not afraid of these fakers. I wish they would try to knock the books from my hands or force me to undress."

"Hold yer horses."

"It would be their funeral, Tex. Not mine."

"Whoa. I know ya can wrestle an elephant. Why don't we kick cyber butt instead."

"Fine. But as soon as I graduate I might have to commit a little assault and battery."

"Not worth it."

"I'm not so sure." Sheridan hung up her phone and set the ringer to vibrate. Inside, the old man sighed. Let him. On the computer she pulled up the website. Since school just got out, she wasn't sure she'd find anyone online. The blog was hip and well organized, which only made the words they posted more criminal. Being mean should never be popular.

Vengeancel: Hey Ribbon, if you're out there. Give me a

shout out.
Nov 15 at 4:12 P.M.

The response was almost instant.

Princess17: who's this?
Nov 15 at 4:12 P.M.

Vengeance1: Where's Ribbon?
Nov 15 at 4:12 P.M.

Princess17: r u lame?
Nov 15 at 4:12 P.M.

Vengeance1: No. Are you?
Nov 15 at 4:12 P.M.

Princess17: who is this?
Nov 15 at 4:12 P.M.

Vengeance1: No one you need to worry about. I'm looking for Ribbon.
Nov 15 at 4:13 P.M.

Princess17: oh yeah?
Nov 15 at 4:13 P.M.

Snap. A pop-up window appeared with the words, "You no longer have access to this site." That was fast. Sheridan signed on with her second account.

Vengeance2: Why'd you shut me off? You scared or something?

Nov 15 at 4:15 P.M.

Snap.

Vengeance3: I'm not going away.
Nov 15 at 4:17 P.M.

Princess17: THIS IS MY SITE. SO GET OFF
Nov 15 at 4:17 P.M.

Snap.

Vengeance4: NO!!!!! I want to know what happened
to my friend Ribbon.
Nov 15 at 4:19 P.M.

Princess17: who cares what you want?
Nov 15 at 4:20 P.M.

Vengeance4: What did she ever do to you?
Nov 15 at 4:20 P.M.

Princess17: she stunk up my school.
Nov 15 at 4:20 P.M.

Got2beGood: yeah, she pissed her pants
Nov 15 at 4:20 P.M.

Princess17: you must be a bed wetter 2.
Nov 15 at 4:20 P.M.

Vengeance4: It takes dung to know dung.
Nov 15 at 4:21 P.M.

Got2beGood: no problem, now that she's gone, we can flush u 2.
Nov 15 at 4:21 P.M.

Snap. Sheridan burst into laughter. This was more fun than she'd thought. The man next to her scowled. Oops. She covered her mouth with her hand to let him know she'd be quieter next time. Of the twelve computers in the library, only four were occupied. Besides her and the old guy, a soccer mom sat next to a college student across from her. Sheridan opened a magazine and pretended to read as she watched the screen banter for a minute, then used her fifth sign-on.

Vengeance5: Ribbon. Don't listen to these freaks. You're awesome.
Nov 15 at 4:26 P.M.

Snap.

Vengeance6: What's wrong princess? Lose your crown?
Nov 15 at 4:28 P.M.

Princess17: get off the line.
Nov 15 at 4:28 P.M.

Vengeance6: You scared? You're a bunch of babies hiding behind fake names. If I were to meet you I'd bet everything about you is fake from your hair to your toe-jammed pedicures.
Nov 15 at 4:28 P.M.

Princess17: girls, call me at home, we've got some trash to burn.
Nov 15 at 4:28 P.M.

Vengeance6: bye.
Nov 15 at 4:29 P.M.

Snap.

Vengeance7: I'm still here.
Nov 15 at 4:31 P.M.

Hottie-girl: who r u?
Nov 15 at 4:32 P.M.

Vengeance7: Why? Are you Ribbon?
Nov 15 at 4:32 P.M.

Hottie-girl: no way. get a clue.
Nov 15 at 4:32 P.M.

Vengeance7: I'm trying to.
Nov 15 at 4:33 P.M.

Blue_eyesl01: look she's gone, k? leave us alone.
Nov 15 at 4:33 P.M.

Sheridan checked her list. The Princess' real name was Courtney. Some chick named Madeline was the Hottie-girl, Blue-eyesl01 was named Ashley. Maybe she was the Ashley Ribbon mentioned in her journal. Tex said that girl hadn't been on the site for days. It could be remorse.

> **Vengeance7:** I don't care about you guys. I just want to talk to Ribbon and I'll leave your smutty site for good.
> Nov 15 at 4:34 P.M.

> **Hottie-girl:** then check your sewer, no one here cares about that anymore, it's old news.
> Nov 15 at 4:34 P.M.

> **Vengeance7:** I care.
> Nov 15 at 4:35 P.M.

The cursor on the screen flashed.

> **Vengeance7:** Did you hear me? Ribbon, if you're listening, I care.
> Nov 15 at 4:36 P.M.

> **Hottie-girl:** go somewhere else and do it.
> Nov 15 at 4:36 P.M.

The princess must be on the phone still, since Sheridan hadn't been blocked yet. They were probably trying to find out who the sign-on belonged to. It was nice to know Tex was somewhere in this cyber world with her. These creeps weren't backing down. Who knew what they were capable of?

Sheridan took a deep breath and tapped the heels of her leather flats together. It wasn't over the top to think these twits had hurt Ribbon. They could have jumped her. There was an old movie where some kids pranked a call to a number from the phone book and said, "I know who you are and I saw what you've done." The random man had actually killed someone. Maybe she could fool these jerks into saying more than they wanted to.

Vengeance7: Then the rumors must be true.
Nov 15 at 4:38 P.M.

Hottie-girl: what rumors?
Nov 15 at 4:38 P.M.

Vengeance7: You guys did something to her. I know you did something to her. The reason I can't find her is because you probably killed her.
Nov 15 at 4:38 P.M.

The chat log stayed blank for a full minute.

Vengeance7: Killers. Murderers. You're dead next. Ribbon might be hiding in heaven, but you're the ones going to hell.
Nov 15 at 4:39 P.M.

Snap. Okay, so her majesty was still reading. But why didn't they deny it? Her heart began to pound so loud she looked over to see if the noise bothered the man next to her.

Vengeance8: welcome back princess. You ready to confess?
Nov 15 at 4:43 P.M.

No response.

Vengeance8: Tell you what I'm going to do. I'm going to make sure Ribbon gets justice. Watch your back.
Nov 15 at 4:44 P.M.

Princess17: i didn't do anything, you fat cow. And when i find you Ribbon won't be the only one dead.
Nov 15 at 4:45 P.M.

Snap.

Vengeance9: Where is she.
Nov 15 at 4:47 P.M.

Princess17: gone, no loss, now what can i do to make u disappear?
Nov 15 at 4:47 P.M.

Vengeance9: Confess.
Nov 15 at 4:47 P.M.

Princess17: what r you a cop? confess to what?
Nov 15 at 4:47 P.M.

Vengeance9: To killing my friend.
Nov 15 at 4:47 P.M.

Sheridan lifted her fingers from the keyboard. Please let it not be true. Even if Ribbon still breathed, something had died in the last journal entry Sheridan had read.

Vengeance9: Look, Princess, or should I say

Courtney, you are done. I will haunt this site until you give me what I want. Ribbon deserves respect.
Nov 15 at 4:50 P.M.

Snap. Tension tingled in her fingers. She was right. These creeps did something horrible to Ribbon. Hard as she tried to stop the images of movies she'd seen of people in remote places with baseball bats and a body in a trunk, she only had one more sign-on, so she needed to choose her last words carefully.

Vengeance10: The same goes for Helen and Maddie and the rest of your gang, I'm off to tell the world what you did. But don't worry, I'll be back before you can miss me.
Nov 15 at 4:53 P.M.

Princess17: u have nothing on me. and i'm here to tell you vengeance burns both ways.
Nov 15 at 4:53 P.M.

Snap.

Chapter 23

It wasn't until Tinkerbell's loud laugh that Ashley noticed her on the computer across from her. She crouched lower into her seat. At first she thought the new girl had followed her into the library. Then she noticed the synchronization between Tinkerbell's keystrokes and those of the vengeance sign-ons.

When the new girl accused them of killing Ribbon, Ashley swallowed her gum. Mom used to tell her the wad would never digest and clog up her insides. Hate was the same. As soon as you swallow it, it becomes a permanent part of you. There it remained locked in your gut, unmoving and dead.

As the chat conversation ended, the gurgle in Ashley's stomach became a growl. She looked up to see if anyone heard. The words typed by the short blonde were true. At least five times Ashley typed the words, "I'm sorry," into the small, white box on her screen. And five times she deleted it without hitting enter. Courtney and everyone in her crowd knew she was Blue_eyes101. If she typed the apology, she'd face more retaliation. The new girl had the advantage of anonymity.

Good thing Ashley went casual after gym. Tinkerbell would have to be an undercover detective to recognize Ashley with her curly hair, glasses, and make-up-free face. Even the San Diego State sweatshirt she'd pulled on provided a change from their earlier encounter.

Ashley clicked the X to close out of the instant messenger. Not that it mattered. Turning off the machine didn't erase the words. A stabbing pain pinched her heart. The new piece of mango-flavored gum didn't refresh her spirit. Hate lived perpetually in cyberspace. The accusations remained posted for anyone to read. Stinging prickles pulsed through her veins. A tight ache constricted her lungs. Bold, black-and-white smut filled the World Wide Web with the filth they'd spread. The ugly words were read religiously and blindly believed. Powerful enough to make Ribbon do the impossible.

It was nice to see Courtney get a bit of her own back. No one had ever contested what she did, let alone stood up for Ribbon. But how did the new girl know about Ribbon in the first place? Ashley worked the gum with her back molars. At the beginning, Vengeance had asked for the dead girl, but at the end she'd flat out accused them of murder. And why couldn't the gang stop her? When Courtney asked the girls to call it was code for "trace that log on." But that didn't happen. Tinkerbell stayed on the site as long as she'd wanted. This was the first time someone successfully hacked into Courtney's space unidentified. And the first time anyone had used real names. Maybe this new girl actually was a detective.

Oh man. Maybe she was undercover. Ashley had seen that on *Dateline*. The new girl stood up. She was so short. Could she actually be an investigator in disguise?

Ashley watched the Screensaver twist the library's name into odd angles. Ribbon's father might have hired her. Mrs. Barber wanted the suicide to stay secret, but maybe the police were involved. Nobody at school had made an announcement. It wasn't in the newspaper.

The gang *had* killed Ribbon. The innocent misfit had been tortured to death over the last few years. A daisy dropped into a locker would never make up for Ashley's part in that killing. She was ready to be free of it. But was she brave enough to die herself?

Across the room, the new girl weaved her way to the exit. Ashley grabbed her things. Regardless of the consequences, she had to follow.

Chapter 24

Sheridan bumped a couple of people on her way out of the library. The autumn sun hung over the palm-treed horizon. Why did people have to be so evil? She punched in Tex's name in her phone. He answered right away.

"Jumpin' jokers! That was tree-mendous."

"Tex, my hands are shaking."

"Don't fret. They won't find out who ya are."

"That's not it." She wished one of them would try to come after her. "What if it's true?" Sheridan swallowed. "What if she is dead?"

"We'll call the law."

"A lot of good that did in Yuba County."

"You gotta have some faith."

"In grown-ups? Never." The only thing she needed to do now was catch her bus. "I'll call you later." The chat room confrontation proved to be pointless. These brats couldn't have cared less. The sooner she found out what happened to Ribbon the better. It just couldn't be too late. The girl was too real to her.

The number 923 was at the stop across the street. Sheridan waved her hands and screamed for the bus to wait. The driver gave her the thumbs up and did the right thing. She hurried across the street.

The folding doors sighed open. Sheridan climbed through while the bus waited for another commuter. In the back, an empty back seat remained vacant for her. She plopped her backpack on the seat by the window so she could sit alone and read Ribbon's journal. But instead of reading the next page, Sheridan flipped to the last entry and fingered the paper. The answer had to be in the last few lines. A clear-white page had three separate lines drawn out in individual paragraphs.

Ribbon IS ugly.

Ribbon IS stupid.

Ribbon SHOULD die.

The letters on the page had lost the joy of the earlier entries. The writing had changed to stiff-lined print. The flowers and colors were gone. Sketched black birds swooped over naked trees.

Sheridan turned back a couple of pages, hoping she was wrong.

Chapter 25

Words crowd the air in my room like a flock of bats. They pick at my soul, leaving gaping wounds. Some of the words stick to the cuts like leeches sucking and gathering life from me. Others burrow in like wood ticks and scab the surface.

Sometimes I see the words on my skin and face. I dig and claw to remove them, but it is too late—they're too numerous to fight. They swarm all over me. Three-dimensional words, tangible and thick. They cover me like an extra layer of skin. They are invisible enough to fool my parents, who blame my silence on adolescent hormones. My new coat is thick and heavy and cold like leather, but it fits tight and tough around me. When I touch my own skin I no longer feel anything.

Kind or loving words drip off me like water on plastic. But all the hate is absorbed. Each ugly phrase deepens my resolve and makes my decision easier.

The latest posting on the school website has a picture of me hanging from a noose. The animated image swings back and forth *so* peacefully, I think I'm ready. Ready to escape.

Chapter 26

The journal dropped to Sheridan's lap in slow motion. "Ribbon, no," she whispered to herself. This wonderful girl couldn't be dead. It took a conscious thought to breathe. It was only a game in the library, accusing those girls of killing Ribbon. But was it true? Tex had spent the last forty-eight hours searching for the girl, and he wasn't able to find her. Her parents hadn't moved, and there were no transfer records indicating she was at another school.

Hopefully, if she made a suicide attempt, it failed. Ribbon could be safe in the psych-ward of a hospital somewhere. Better that than dead. Trees and houses blurred past the window. Sheridan rubbed the cover of Ribbon's journal with the tips of her fingers. Those girls at the school needed to pay. No matter where Ribbon was now. They couldn't get away with this.

This couldn't be the end of Ribbon's story.

The bus turned into Sheridan's neighborhood. As it approached her street, she signaled for the vehicle to make the next stop. The brakes squealed, and the bus jerked to a rest. She stepped off in a daze. The sadness of the situation yanked so deep in her gut her tear ducts were dry. She pulled out her phone.

"Hi, Nina, I just got off the bus. I'll be home in a minute."

"Great."

Nina couldn't know, nothing was great.

Sheridan closed the phone and headed up the hill. This place was the best she'd ever stayed. She didn't want to leave. But was it worth letting those idiots continue running the school? Her fingers tightened on Ribbon's journal. She hugged it to her chest. The old nursery rhyme about sticks and stones was a lie. The hags on the front steps needed to pay. The princess needed to be dethroned. The only way to do that would be a good, old-fashioned punch-fest. The only language those creeps spoke. Ribbon needed an avenger.

She rounded the corner. A dog assaulted a chain-link fence, and Sheridan almost jumped out of her skin. Stupid dog. She caught her breath and glared at the obnoxious pug.

Okay, he was just doing his job, but man, he'd almost given her a heart attack.

It wasn't until she neared the end of the circle that she appreciated the noisy bark. The vocal canine let her know someone was following her. Please let it be one of those life-sized Barbies. She dropped one hand from Ribbon's journal and clenched her fingers into a fist.

Chapter 27

A shley's muscles still ached from the beat-down last night, but she kept moving. Tinkerbell had stopped when the dumb dog started barking. The new girl waited with fists clenched. *Let's get it over with.* Within two steps they were face to face.

"Who are you?" Ashley started.

"You followed me."

"How do you know Ribbon?" Ashley put her hands on her hips so the girl wouldn't see them tremble.

"Who are *you?*"

"I saw you at the library on the Internet."

"It's a free world." Tinkerbell shrugged.

"You wrote about Ribbon."

"What's it to you?" Tinkerbell let her backpack drop to the ground.

This was it. Ashley was too sore to fight, but she couldn't keep wondering. It was time to know even if it meant more bruises. "How did you know Ribbon killed herself?"

The girl unclenched her fist.

The dog started barking behind them. Ashley turned to see an afternoon jogger jump back from the fence and curse the dog. The man picked up his stride and bounced past them.

The new girl stood unmoved. The breeze wrestled Ashley's hair. In the last two weeks, she'd questioned every choice she'd ever made. Life had become so confusing she had no idea what to do now. One thing was for sure—she couldn't trust her thoughts or feelings. Courtney wasn't worth all the trouble she caused. Neither was a hurricane, but it was equally unmanageable.

Tinkerbell's posture deflated. "So, she did it?"

"You didn't know?" The foundations Ashley had built were crumbling beneath her. What was solid wavered. Nothing in life made sense. Not one thing. From the moment Ribbon ended her own life, the world hung purposeless in the universe.

"What does Ribbon have to do with *you*. Huh? You follow me here because you want to talk about Ribbon?" The new girl stepped toward Ashley, forcing her to back down. "I think you know what happened. And now you are trying to find out *why* she killed herself?"

Ashley braced herself for the pain. The attack in the park couldn't appease her guilt, but maybe a couple hard punches from Tinkerbell would. She deserved nothing less.

"You want to know why Ribbon's dead? You did it." Tinkerbell pointed her finger in Ashley's face. "If you attend North Harbor High, you killed her. You and every other coward at that school. If you didn't harass her personally, you sat by and watched." Fury filled the girl's cheeks, and her eyes bit through Ashley like a laser.

"And if you saw me on the Internet then you must have been on there yourself. If you want to know who to blame, try looking in the mirror."

Then she turned away so fast Ashley flinched.

She'd thought it. She'd felt it. But to hear someone confirm it made it real. Ashley held her gum inside the corner of her right cheek. The breeze continued to blow and Ashley couldn't move. Her feet were glued to the sidewalk.

Guilty.

The best friend Ribbon ever had.

Guilty.

The worst enemy Ribbon ever had.

Guilty.

Tinkerbell stormed away. Ashley stood in the truth of the new girl's accusation. A strand of hair blew into her eyes. The jogger made his lap around the circle. He loped past her. The dog complained. No matter what she did or said, tomorrow Ribbon Barber would still be dead.

Chapter 28

After dinner, Sheridan hammered the keys on her bedroom computer. The words rushed across the screen without correction. For thirty minutes she kept her head down and watched her fingers hit the letters. Pouring words from her heart to the page was therapy. She was full of outrage and sorrow. How could they? How could any of them? Those plastic stick-figures, including the curly-haired brunette, had no right to stalk the halls and crush anyone who came near. They were a gang of brainless bullies standing on the front steps like they owned the school, and running over anyone they wanted to hurt on the Internet.

How dare that witch follow her home. She should have punched her. She should have crushed her like the insect she was. What a joke. Did they really think this world was made for them? Did they honestly believe they could do whatever they wanted without consequences? Forget about sticks or stones or fists or kicks. Words killed Ribbon. And they didn't materialize on their own. They started with the twisted, immature thoughts of selfish, judgmental idiots who defined what was permissible in their warped, backward world. Was Ribbon's family crazy? Maybe, but so what. That didn't give these jerks a right to condemn her. To attack and destroy her.

And where were the teachers at North Harbor High? Where were the adults? Sure, Sheridan didn't trust grown-ups because of the events on the farm. But when did they decide to turn their backs on their responsibility to their community? This whole thing was an insult. The authorities had ignored the vicious website and the unjust actions of so many. What happened to a society which disregards an entire generation? Who cared, right? The effects wouldn't be felt for twenty years. Let another generation deal with it. Not my problem. Whatever. Well, Sheridan made it her problem and kept typing until her brain ran out of rage.

When she finally took a breath, the page was full of words underlined by the spell-checker. Time to edit and fix. Time to include the names. Courtney, Ashley, even Miss Jones, the counselor who had played a part. Guilty, guilty, guilty. These people would pay.

When her fingers tired, she paced the room. The article was over ten pages, practically a book. That didn't matter. The school paper would never print it. She would polish it until it could be sent to the local newspaper or even some tabloid television show. This needed to be announced from the tallest mountain.

Tex would find a way if there was one. Sheridan paced over to her backpack when her cell phone in the side pocket started to vibrate. She reached in and pulled it out.

"Where were you?" he said before she could speak.

"Hi, Tex." Sheridan sank into the beanbag.

"Don't you 'Hi, Tex' me. I've been trying ta call ya for hours."

"Sorry. I set my phone to vibrate."

"Well, a brother worries about his sister."

"Thanks." That ray of sunshine calmed Sheridan's mood. "Tex, Ribbon's dead."

"Now, don't jump to conclusions. It's good to put them girls on the run, but don't panic."

"I'm not. One of them followed me home." Sheridan leaned back onto the shifting sack.

"Whoa."

"Yeah. She asked me how I knew Ribbon had killed herself." Sheridan studied the paint on the ceiling. The words still hurt. She rubbed her eyes to keep from crying.

"Suicide?"

"Yeah." Sheridan choked back the word along with the tears. She kicked her shoes into the corner. "I've been sitting here, writing an article for the school newspaper. I've got to get back at them. Someone needs to speak for Ribbon. Even if she's not here."

"Man. I'm so sorry."

"Do you think it will work?" Please say yes. Please say there is something they could do.

Tex was quiet for a moment. "Maybe. But what if we serve 'em a little Yuba County grub?"

"What do you mean?" Sheridan leaned forward. The chair morphed beneath her.

"A few flyers."

"That's your big idea?" Sheridan wanted to punch him. "Listen, dummy. San Diego is too big. It would take a year to staple posters to the telephone poles around here."

"I ain't talking 'bout littering the town. I'm talking 'bout the school. They do it all the time at elections."

"I'm not running for office."

"Do ya want help or not?" Tex's voice came through the phone so loud Sheridan had to pull it away from her ear.

"Calm down, dude."

"I will when ya stop being so stubborn. Think 'bout it. You can tape their pictures on the walls in school, stick 'em on the windshields of cars."

Sheridan allowed a full grin to stretch across her face. "Embarrass them at school. I love it."

"Yup." Tex was excited. "Give me an hour then check yer email."

"Sounds great. Too bad we don't own a blimp."

The warmth of being part of a family flowed through her. She missed Elsie. The next time she talked to her caseworker she would ask to speak to the younger foster girl and her other brothers and sisters. The best way to have a family was to love the ones she'd been given.

Those twits deserved to get back ten times worse than what they gave. The first item on her list—lay low—was now permanently crossed off. At this point she was ready to sacrifice graduation if it meant justice for Ribbon. She wasn't thrilled to think she might get kicked out of Nina and Joe's. But, so what? Her eighteenth birthday was right around the corner. Why worry about the inevitable? Nope. She'd graduate regardless, even if it was from a group home on the Internet.

The email from Tex came with a total of twelve different flyers that looked like wanted posters. The faces were made up of distorted caricatures, but the actual names of the girls, Courtney, Helen, and Ashley, were bold and easy to read. He'd used gothic script to spell out the words killer and murderer.

Now she needed a plan to get them printed and hung. She had almost three thousand dollars in cash hidden in the head of a plastic doll she'd had since she was small. It was her personal stash. Her own doll-head savings account. Nina would turn purple if she knew Sheridan was already good with money. Tex had helped her find ways to make money in Marysville. One thing always looming over a foster child's head was their eighteenth birthday. Some foster folks kept their kids while they went to college. Nina and Joe might just be that type. But either way, it was best to be prepared.

Sheridan wouldn't have a problem going to a twenty-four-hour Kinkos. But how would she get into North Harbor High? It would take forever to hang twelve hundred flyers around the school. Thirty minutes passed before she remembered the first friend she'd made at the school. The answer to her problem was José Talmadge.

Chapter 29

Ashley eventually moved. Her subconscious carried her from Tinkerbell's neighborhood to Ribbon's church. Somehow the concrete bench did not crumble under the weight she now carried.

Each blade of grass remained stationary as her vision blurred. Thoughts and words tumbled together in her mind. Birds chirped at her as happy images of her elementary school friend collided with Ribbon's tortured expressions.

Ribbon's smile
Ribbon's frown
Courtney's smile
Tinkerbell's frown
Courtney
Helen
Ribbon
Maddie
Courtney
Ribbon
Vengencel

Ribbon
Princess17
Ribbon
got2beGood
Ribbon
Blue_eyes101
Ribbon
Ribbon
Ribbon
Rib bon
Ribb on

The sun fought the horizon until Ashley found the strength to leave the empty church. The early evening was silent but not eerie. Resolve had settled into her heart. Possibly for the first time in her entire life, she knew exactly what she needed to do.

There was no sense of urgency when she got home, just purpose.

She started by downloading some of the more vicious chat room conversations onto a flash drive.

An Internet search provided the story of a girl who had been bullied to death in Massachusetts. Google helped her find the story of the Missouri mom who pretended to be a teen boy in order to taunt her daughter's rival to suicide. That woman was not convicted. Ashley would be. She'd make sure of it. With the copies of evidence printed in separate purple folders, she drove over to Ribbon's house. In the past, she'd always walked. This time the trip was fast. Light from the window created obscure shadows on the path. Ashley marched past them and knocked on the door. Professor Barber answered.

"Karen," he called and started to walk away, but Ashley stopped him.

"No sir, I need to talk to you."

Professor Barber faced her with indignation surging through his eyes. Mrs. Barber appeared behind him, wiping her hands on a rag. "Ashley, hi, what are you doing here?"

"I need to talk to your husband," she responded, not taking her eyes off Professor Barber. He hadn't moved from his spot, so she continued. "I've come to confess."

"Excuse me?" He leaned his weight on one foot.

"I know who killed Ribbon. I know, and I'm going to the police." Ashley flinched as Professor Barber's posture tightened.

"Wait." Mrs. Barber stepped in front of her husband and gently touched his arm. "Ribbon killed herself, and we are dealing with that."

"Read it." Ashley thrust the folder toward them. "Read it."

The muscles in Mr. Barber's forearm flinched, and his teeth came together in a tight grip. "Leave us alone."

"I'm going to the police." Ashley and the professor stared hard at each other. "Ribbon deserves justice. I just thought you should know."

"Give me a break." His words pushed their way through his teeth. Their eyes met. "You're not here to confess. You've come to blame us. Right? This is nothing short of an opportunity to condemn our beliefs. You want to make our environmental lifestyle a crime. Let me tell you now, Ribbon didn't die because of neglect."

He pounded his fists on the door frame. "I fight to protect this dying planet." He swallowed. "My whole life I've tried to make this world a better place. I've worked hard to ensure your children's children will have rain forests. I'm so sick of this place I could scream. How can you come to me as if I didn't have a father's heart? As if I hadn't spent the last two weeks in this empty house. If I'm guilty of anything, it is not protecting my daughter from the likes of you. You selfish brat, you can take your evidence and get off my property."

He yanked the folder from her and chucked it in the air. Pages rained down at Ashley's feet. Her heart throbbed. "You're right," she whispered. "We killed her, not you. We killed her with our words. We killed her with our hate, with our ignorance and stupidity."

"What are you talking about?" His eyes narrowed.

"Please understand, I never wanted this to happen."

"What did you do?"

He didn't know. Of course not. Ribbon never told anyone.

"She was bullied. At the school. Every day."

"And you've come to clear your conscience?" He kicked at the papers. "You filthy, selfish brat. Garbage doesn't evaporate."

"Ben, stop."

He didn't. "When you toss your trash, it contaminates everyone else in the world. Whether it's paper or plastic or *words*. You want to feel better about yourself? Try keeping some of your mess inside, why don't you?"

"I can't." She didn't mean to raise her voice. But this wasn't about them. "I'm terrified, don't you understand?"

"Of what?"

Ashley looked into the eyes of the grieving father. All the wishing in the world would not get him to understand her motives and would not relieve the brokenness in her heart. She hugged herself.

"Tell me." Sarcasm oozed through his tone.

"I'm afraid that if I don't fix this soon, I'll give up the way Ribbon did."

Chapter 30

I no longer carry books. It's easier to be pushed than to have someone slap stuff out of my hands. Besides, books contain words, and words are evil.

Never mind. That's stupid.

Words aren't evil. They separate us from animals. There's a yellow lab next door named George. He barks at everyone who passes, except me. Mostly because I played with him when he was a puppy.

The other day I stopped by the fence and petted George. The dog wagged his tail. I said to him, "You are such a stupid dog." My tone was sweet and kind and his tail thumped against the ground.

Then I spoke in a scolding voice, "You are a very good dog. A very, very, good dog." His ears flattened and his tail sagged. I couldn't stand to see him that way and I changed my tone. Because it's the tone that hurts. Words are powerful, but they are only the dynamite; tone lights the fuse.

It's not like I really want to die. What I want is to stop hurting. What I want is to end the pain. The problem is that there isn't a medicine in the world that can make the nasty lies and the awful truths go away. I don't want to give up. But nothing can change the tone in the voices that surround me. Including the ones in my head.

Chapter 31

Sheridan's first call was to the twenty-four-hour Kinko's. That was easy. One hundred copies of twelve different flyers would dent her meager savings, but it was worth it. Ribbon had a right to be heard.

Now came the hard part. She had to find José Talmadge's phone number. It was a big stretch to think the janitor would help her trash the school, but the guy was her only hope. She'd just have to convince him.

There were only seven Talmadge listings in the white pages. And only one with the Spanish first name, José. Sheridan wiped the sweat from her hands and punched the seven-digit number into her cell phone.

A gruff voice answered on the other end after three rings. *"Hola."*

"Hello. Is this José Talmadge, the janitor at North Harbor High School?"

"Si." He puffed out a heavy sigh. "What's broken now?"

"Oh, nothing."

"Then what you call me for?"

"Mr. Talmadge, my name is Sheridan. I go to North Harbor High School."

"How you get this number?"

"I'm not calling to cause problems. I'm calling to thank you."

"For what?"

"For rescuing me from my locker a couple of days ago."

"Oh." His tone turned friendly. "The little blonde. How are you, *mija?* Did you unfold okay?"

"Yes, sir." Sheridan relaxed. "Thanks to you."

"Good. Good."

"Well, sir, I was hoping you could help me do something."

"*¿Qué?*" He sounded apprehensive again.

"The kids at North Harbor aren't that nice."

"*Sí.*"

"They bully not only the kids, but they also seem to run the school. I have to be honest. I'm mad. I don't like what they do to new kids like me. Besides, they also torment nice people like you."

"Go on."

He was still listening—that was good. "I don't know how many times you needed to clean the locker that was given to me. But even the one time you cleaned it for me was too much."

An inpatient sigh huffed through the phone. "So, what you want?"

"I want to go to the school tonight and hang some flyers on the walls with pictures of some of the kids who are guilty. The doors are probably locked. And if I try to do it while the school is open, those kids will stop me."

"No way. I can't do this thing."

"Please, don't hang up. This is really important."

"To who? Sounds like a bunch of paper I have to clean up later."

"I promise I'll help you. I'll do whatever you need. I have to do this for the girl who had the locker before me."

"Ah, Ribbon. Didn't she transfer?"

"No."

"Where is she?"

"She killed herself." Sheridan rocked back and forth on the bed. That was all she had. The total of her ammo spent in three quick words.

Mr. Talmadge didn't say anything for a long time. But she would wait as long as it took. The news slugged her in the gut when she first heard it, and the journal had given her some warning. Maybe this janitor remembered Ribbon as a living, breathing person.

He eventually said, "Meet me at the school at eleven o'clock."

"You've got it." Sheridan checked the clock. A couple of hours should be enough time. She tossed the phone on her bed and headed to the closet.

What kind of shoes do people wear to a B & E?

Chapter 32

Less than a handful of cars occupied the police station lot. Ashley slipped a package of gum from her purse and put it in her pocket. This might be the last time she could chew the different fruit flavors she wanted. Did prisoners get gum? Probably, but maybe not the Trident brand she liked. A swarm of hornets battered her insides. She had no idea what it would be like to be locked up. Even when Dad grounded her, she still went outside to go to school. Freedom ended for her tonight.

Tall palm trees silhouetted the night sky. This could be her last view of nature for a long time. Deep breaths didn't help. And neither would crying. She patted her cheeks and then rubbed her palms together. Time to go.

The concrete stairs to the police station were lighted. Ashley climbed the steps to the entrance. A firm yank on the handle didn't budge the door. She tugged on it a second time. Locked. This wasn't good. If she didn't do this tonight, fear would keep her away forever. Besides, why would a police station be closed at night?

She cupped her hands and peered into the glass. A beam illuminated the floor beneath a closed door deep in the back. Should she knock? Painted letters on the window indicated the office hours were weekdays from 8:00 A.M. to 5:00 P.M. Below that, Ashley found the after-hour instructions and the intercom on the side wall. She pushed the button and waited.

This was hard. She squeezed the purple folder. Why didn't they answer? Certainly, crimes were committed at night. What if someone was attacking her? What if it was an emergency? Of course, in that case she'd call 9-1-1. Maybe that's what she should have done. A police car could come to her, sirens blasting announcing they'd found another low-life criminal. The world needed to know. She pushed the button again. Come on. She didn't know if she had the strength to wait or come back.

"How can I help you?" A voice crackled from the speaker.

"I need to speak to a police officer."

"About what?"

Ashley let her gum rest in her cheek then said, "I've killed someone."

A buzz sounded, and the latch on the glass door clicked. The person on the other side of the intercom said, "Come in."

When she pulled on the handle this time it yielded. Lights brightened the dim room from a now-open doorway. The dark shadow of an officer stretched across the floor outlined in a disfigured yellow rectangle. Ashley hugged the evidence. She shuffled past the counter with Plexiglas windows where people came during the day. Ghostly witnesses remained silent in the empty waiting room chairs.

"Come on in." The man in uniform propped the door open with his back. His right hand rested on his hip. Well, actually it was on his gun. Ashley didn't see anger or judgment in the dark eyes of the black police officer. He smiled. Maybe he thought this whole thing was a prank. Either way, he didn't take his hand off his gun.

In the room, most of the people wore uniforms and looked up long enough to notice her. The door closed behind her and that was it. She was in, and when she left she'd be in handcuffs.

"My name is Officer Paul Moore." He smiled at her. "I understand you want to confess to something."

"Yes."

"Before we do that, I need some basic information. What's your name?"

"Ashley Nobel." They'd probably put a number under her mug shot like on *America's Most Wanted*.

"Do you have any identification?"

Ashley set the purple folder on the closest desk and reached into her purse for her wallet. From her peripheral vision she noticed another officer studying her. Officer Moore wrote down her information on a large, yellow pad.

"Right this way." The congenial officer returned her ID and led her to a hallway on the left. He stopped at a vending machine. "Can I get you something to drink?"

"No, thank you." The thought of carbonated bubbles in her already chaotic stomach didn't sound good. She'd stick with gum.

Ashley twisted her hair around one finger as coins clunked into the machine. A diet coke landed with a thud into the tray. The officer carried the drink in his left hand with the yellow note pad tucked under his arm. His right hand stayed close to his side. He was going to ask for her story and then put her in jail. The whole thing felt surreal, but right. Besides the nerves, she was glad to know this would all be over soon.

At the third left in a narrow hallway, the officer opened the door to an interrogation room. "After you." He stood like a gentleman on a date and let her enter first. "Have a seat."

There wasn't a two-way mirror the way she'd seen on TV. Instead, a camera in the corner captured the small table and three chairs in the room. Ashley sat down and started to flick the purple folder in her lap.

"Our conversation is being recorded." The plastic on the legs of the chair scraped against the floor as he sat down.

"Okay." Ashley was ready.

"What did you come to tell me?" He made direct eye contact with Ashley as he pulled a pen from his pocket.

"I killed someone." Ashley maintained eye contact with the officer for less than a full second. Embarrassment forced her to look at the gray tile floor. She rubbed her arms to battle back a shiver. The idea of being locked in a cell with no windows sucked. But she deserved it. Ribbon's freedom had been taken from her. Shouldn't Ashley suffer the same or worse? That's justice. Plus, it would bring life a little bit back into balance.

"Was this someone you knew?" He popped the top of his diet drink. Fizz escaped from the opening.

"Yes. She was my best friend in elementary school."

"What's her name?"

"Ribbon Barber."

He wrote down her name in bold, black letters. "And why did you kill her?" The voice of Officer Moore didn't fluctuate with each question. He was being way too nice to her. There was no bright spotlight in Ashley's eyes. No scowl on the cop's face.

"I didn't mean to."

"Tell me how you killed her."

"It's all in here." Ashley put the folder on the table and slid it closer to the officer.

"Can you give me the highlights?" The officer opened the purple cover and scanned the first page.

"These are copies from the Internet." Ashley didn't know how to explain it. What seemed obvious to her at the Barber's house didn't flow as smoothly here. She gnawed at the gum in her mouth. "Ribbon killed herself a couple of weeks ago. She did it because she was being bullied by me and a bunch of people at the school."

For the first time all night, Officer Moore's expression changed. Instead of mellow confidence, his eyebrows folded into an expression of being unsure. Ashley gripped her knees. "We have picked on her every day since seventh grade. We've called her names and hit her." She puffed out a breath. "Everything you can imagine has been done to this girl."

"We who?"

"Everyone at North Harbor High."

"You want me to arrest an entire school for the suicide of one girl?" The officer leaned his elbows on his knees and interlaced his chocolate colored fingers.

"No." Ashley shook her head. "Just me."

"Why just you?"

"Because I was her best friend. All those other kids didn't know her. I did. If I had continued to be her friend, she'd still be alive."

"You don't know that. Suicide is a complicated thing."

"She trusted me, and I turned on her. She had no one to go to, and we still went at her. Every day. Do you understand that? We tortured her, and she finally gave up and killed herself."

"I'm sorry, but unless you gave her the gun or fed her some poison, it's hard to prove a connection."

"I'm here to confess. Isn't that enough?"

"I don't think so."

"Look." Ashley reached for the folder and pulled out a couple pages from the back. "Other people are being arrested for this kind of stuff. You need to arrest me." She handed him the news reports from Massachusetts and Missouri.

"It doesn't work like that."

"What do you mean?" Ashley started to shake. "Ribbon's dead because of me. I need to go to jail."

"Listen. Before I can arrest you, I have to verify the facts and make sure what you've brought me is true. Besides, by your own admission, she killed herself."

"But we drove her to it."

"I'm not so sure."

"Huh?" Ashley started to tremble. "What kind of police station is this? Don't you want to solve crimes? This is crazy. I did a horrible thing."

"We do want to stop the bad guys." He stood up. "I'm just not sure you're one of them. Tell you what, I'll follow-up with the district attorney. Their office decides if there is enough evidence to arrest you. That's all I can do. For now, go on home and get some sleep. I promise I'll contact you when I find out something. Okay?"

He was one hundred percent wrong. She was a horrible person and didn't deserve time or consideration. A confession shouldn't be this hard.

Chapter 33

The bright lights from the twenty-four-hour Kinko's faded into residential dimness. Homes were closed and dark. The time on Sheridan's phone indicated 10:53 P.M. The walk didn't take as long as she'd thought. The brick school was creepy in the streetlight's glow. Sheridan imagined the soundtrack from *Rocky*. It encouraged her as she approached the front entrance. But which door would the janitor have left unlocked for her?

Flood lights showered the front entrance. Anyone driving down the street would see her enter that way. The traffic wasn't heavy, but there were enough cars to make it impossible to run up and try it. This time it wasn't the gang she wanted to avoid—more like the police.

Later they could all speculate about who did this. They might even catch her, but she needed to postpone her thought long enough to wallpaper the school with the names of these cows. These hags needed a dose of public humiliation.

The campus seemed larger in the dark. She should have asked Mr. Talmadge for a cell phone number or given him hers. North Harbor was a big school with a lot of doors. What if she couldn't find him? The two and a half boxes of neon colored paper in her backpack shifted as she adjusted the heavy weight with a shrug. Better try the back doors first.

A cloudless sky stretched past the tall palm trees. Random stars and a thin moon glared down on Sheridan as she headed toward the shadows in the back of the school. The soft soles of her sneakers sunk into the grass. The side door was invisible in the dark-covered overhang. These jerks had to pay, but she didn't want to be jumped by some drunk bum who decided to sleep it off on the steps of the school. There was no choice but to go for it. She cleared her throat as loudly as possible and waited to see if the shadows shifted. Nothing moved. The only sound she could hear was her own heartbeat. She climbed the dark stairway. The door didn't budge.

This idea was mad crazy. She could get herself into bigger trouble than she planned. It was one thing to have a handful of immature twits on your case, but it was another to be tackled in a dark alley by a mugger. Or worse.

Her plan obviously had potholes. She slipped down the steps and rounded a flowering shrub. Maybe she should wait for Mr. Talmadge in the parking lot. He wouldn't have walked or taken the bus like she did. Besides, it would be lighted and away from traffic.

She was about to step out of the darkness until she glimpsed a large circle of motorcyclists. There were at least ten guys huddled in the parking lot. This late at night that couldn't be good. The shadows were safer for now. Would those creeps keep the nice janitor away? Maybe he'd already come and gone.

Sheridan hid behind the wall. Did these guys meet

here every night? What would happen if they saw her? She slipped down to the ground with her back against the stone. How would she get into the building now? Mr. Talmadge was a nice man, but he wasn't huge. He couldn't stand up to a motorcycle gang.

The doors leading to the cafeteria were on her left, but she'd have to step into the light from the parking lot to try them. Unless she saw the janitor inside, it wasn't worth the risk. The time on her cell phone shone 11:03 P.M. as more headlights bounced across the wall then stopped. What if that was him? Sheridan peeked at the parking lot, wiping her wet palms together.

Another motorcycle.

The bike's headlight turned off as the engine died down. A short man leaned the bike against its kickstand and removed his helmet.

Mr. Talmadge.

The janitor bumped fists with a couple of the guys. Sheridan stood up. She dusted her hands, still unsure she wanted to enter the lighted area. A large ring jingled from dozens of carved pieces of metal as Mr. Talmadge strutted across the parking lot. She pulled back her shoulders and stepped into the glow.

"Come on, *mija*, let's get this done." The short Latino approached a metal door on the side of the building. The entrance was not available to students. Sheridan followed, still trying to catch her breath. He inserted a key from his large collection and pulled the steel door open. They stepped inside.

The janitor-slash-motorcyclist entered a code into a numeric alarm system. "After you."

"Okay."

Sheridan set her backpack on the floor in the supply

room. The absence of noise and people in a place made for hundreds was eerie. Too much like Alfred Hitchcock. She pushed creepy ideas from her head and unpacked the papers and masking tape. Thank goodness Kinkos was willing to collate this stuff. The flyers for Courtney or Helen or any of the others would be plastered randomly.

The school had three floors. Four hundred pages per floor. That was a lot. Her goal was saturation. But could they actually get it all done in an hour?

"Okay, *mija,* let's see what you have." He picked up a bright pink flyer. A cartoon princess with a scar across her face listed Courtney's name in bold letters at the top. The word *Killer* stretched across the bottom. Mr. Talmadge nodded. "This is very brave. Those *mocosas* don't like people to bother them."

"I know." Sheridan shrugged. "But I can't sit around and do nothing. This is step one. My next step is the newspaper."

"Where do we start?" His crooked grin represented approval to her.

"We could start in the basement. I have four hundred sheets for each floor. We can just go down opposite sides of the hall until we've put them all up."

"I have an idea. Those flyers will be torn down. Let's keep it simple."

"What do you mean?"

"We hang some." He pantomimed the action of taping up a flyer. "But since these *terroristas* like to put things in lockers, we do the same." Then he folded one in half. "Push them into the vents, especially in the boy's gym."

Sheridan liked this man. She nodded, but before she could hand him a box, Mr. Talmadge walked back to the door. He put his thumb and pinkie finger into his mouth and shrilled out a loud whistle. Was he calling for some of those men? She didn't mean to be afraid, but weren't leather-covered gang members dangerous?

"Are those guys coming in here?"

"Not all. Some will stay and watch."

"Oh."

"Don't worry, *mija,* they're good guys." He pointed to the flyers. *"Mucho* work."

"Si," Sheridan said. It was the best idea. Some grown-ups weren't so bad. It might take a motorcycle or two to get them to loosen up. Mr. Talmadge's gang of friends would make the huge chore a cinch.

Chapter 34

Morning hung over North Harbor High like LA fog. Ashley couldn't wait until the DA's office opened. That wouldn't happen until halfway through second period. A few more moments with Courtney would have to be tolerated. But as Ashley approached the entrance, the front steps were empty.

Instead of being relieved, the absence of the crew gave Ashley chills. There was no way the on-line chat from yesterday could have made the gang abandon their turf. In fact, it would have only pissed them off.

Ashley opened the doors to North Harbor High. The chaotic noise inside was amplified by bright-colored flyers. They were impossible to miss. Neon greens and yellows with black-and-white photos of her so-called friends next to the words *Assassin* or *Guilty*.

She tore off a pink one with her name next to the word *Murderer*.

Tinkerbell.

Ashley folded the flyer and stuck it in her pocket. The police department was about to get another witness.

Ashley headed to the darkroom. She'd stay there until 9:00 A.M. She had no desire to watch Courtney's reaction. Better to avoid the drama altogether.

"Where do you think you're going?"

Ashley fell back a couple of steps to avoid crashing into Courtney and Helen. "To my locker," she lied.

"It's in the opposite direction." Helen leaned to one side with her hand on her hip.

A laugh pushed through Ashley's nervous lips.

Courtney grabbed her by the hair. "You think this is funny?"

"No," Ashley whined.

Helen shoved a blue flyer with a picture of Courtney into Ashley's face. "Whoever did this is as nasty as Ribbon. It's disgusting to have people running around who don't bathe or brush their teeth or flush the toilet."

"Ribbon couldn't have done it." Ashley grabbed the hair at the base of her scalp to keep Courtney from pulling it out completely.

"I wasn't talking about her." The dim-wit glared at her.

"Well, I didn't do it." Ashley looked at Courtney. "Why would I put up flyers about myself?"

"'Cause you're an idiot." Helen poked Ashley's shoulder.

Courtney let go. "If they're not from you, where did they come from?"

"Probably that Internet person." Ashley rubbed her scalp.

"Listen, twit." Courtney backed Ashley into the brick wall. Her voice was calm. Ashley didn't mean to, but face to face with the girl who had run the show for so many years made her crumble. "Maddie saw you talking to that new chick last night."

"If she would have listened..." Ashley didn't make eye contact. "She would know I was confronting her."

"Right." Helen stepped forward and slammed Ashley into the locker. "Like the visits you're making to Ribbon's house?"

"Wait, Helen." Courtney backed Helen away with a look. "I want to find out about the new girl. Go ahead, Ashley, tell me what's going on."

"I saw her at the library."

Courtney folded her arms.

"She was on the computer across from me." Nothing mattered anymore. "Remember Vengeance? Well, that's her. She's mad about what happened to Ribbon."

"Why should we believe you?"

"Stop it, Helen," Courtney screamed. Ashley could tell the leader's inner computer buzzed on. "That makes sense."

"I followed her to find out what she was doing."

Courtney pulled out her cell phone. The lead dog was on a new scent. "Listen. Good work." The leader pulled Ashley into a sideways hug. "It will be all right. Daddy will fix it. You're a good friend. Sorry for all the confusion. Okay? I mean, honestly! What kind of world would it be if people get to trash the school and say all kind of lies?"

"Yeah." Helen scrambled to regain position. "That girl makes up some story about Ribbon being dead and decides to go crazy."

"But it's true."

Courtney stopped dialing.

"What's true?" Helen said it at the same time with the same tone.

"Ribbon's not gone. She's dead."

The shock on Courtney's face lasted less than a second. "No way."

Ashley nodded.

"But we didn't kill her," Helen whined.

"Right." Ashley fought to keep any inflection from her voice.

"Whatever." Courtney shook her head as if she could erase what she just heard. "Never mind. Just get busy. Pull down every flyer with my name on it. Don't spend a second removing your own until mine are gone. You got that?"

"No problem."

Helen rolled her eyes and then trailed behind Courtney, who started talking to her dad. Ashley sulked through the halls, pulling down flyers. She'd never hated herself more. Her only consolation was that in a few more hours this would all be over.

Chapter 35

Today I escaped. Mom and Dad were at the university teaching summer courses. I had the house to myself. My chores were done. I curled up on the couch and closed my eyes. The birds on the back porch whistled a random tune and my brain thought I was eight years old again.

The day smelled the same as when Ashley and I pulled a wagon down the bumpy sidewalk and knocked on our neighbors' doors. We were selling stuff our parents gave us. Like a lemonade stand without the lemonade or the stand. Ashley had at least twenty jars of homemade strawberry jam and I had a dozen of Mom's framed quotes.

I enjoyed the memory. I didn't open my eyes for fear I'd chase the moment away with reality. I relaxed into the vision and wished it was real. I even pressed the rewind button a few times. We sold five jars of jam and two framed quotes.

It wasn't time or sleep or sunshine that pulled me out of the vision, but the memory of one of the expressions. "Love means never having to say you're sorry."

I sunk deeper into the couch and cried. The peace ran away and a question stood in its place: What did I ever do to Ashley? Even the tears couldn't answer, although for half an hour they tried.

Chapter 36

"Sheridan."

"Yes." She didn't mean to jump when the teacher called her name. Anticipation had been building in her all morning.

"You need to go to the counselor's office."

The chorus of guttural "ewws" and chuckles coming from the class told her this meant trouble. Whatever. First period or third period, it didn't matter. The curly-haired brunette she met last night might have connected her to the flyers. The witch probably snitched. Sheridan picked up her book and stuffed it into her backpack. Let them do what they wanted. A few flyers were nothing compared to what those haters did.

She accepted the pink slip and headed to Miss Jones' office. All those other girls were probably lined up there. This would be their first look at the enemy. She'd fight for Ribbon's rights. No doubt Nina and Joe had already been called. They might even be sitting there with other parents. It would be a busy day for the counselors.

The residue of her campaign remained in the

hallways. On the wall, masking tape and torn confetti corners matched the shredded posters on the floor. She kicked a balled-up orange page down the corridor until she reached the office. Mr. Talmadge was right about two things. The litter was a no-brainer. But the flyers stuffed in lockers was brilliant. One corner of Sheridan's mouth lifted. Over one hundred colored accusations were folded and hidden in the boys' gym. She picked up a handful of the mess and threw it into a trash can. Thank you, Mr. Talmadge.

The office was quiet as she entered. Even with the open window, the chime in the corner hung limp. The chairs in the waiting area were empty. This didn't make any sense. Where was everyone? She couldn't possibly be the only person in trouble.

"Miss Jones is ready to see you." The studious girl didn't look up from the book she read. There was no offer to escort Sheridan down to the counselors' door this time.

Fine. If nobody in this stinking school wanted to make it right, then Sheridan would rather get kicked out.

"Have a seat." With her hair pulled back into a tight bun, Miss Jones appeared pricklier than she did the other day. Too bad Sheridan didn't tell Tex to make a poster for her too.

"What's up?" Sheridan plopped into the overstuff chair from the first day. The mess from her previous visit continued to rule the office.

"This is your third day, right?" Miss Jones patted the tips of her fingers together.

"Yeah." Sheridan leaned forward with impatience.

"Is there anything we need to talk about?"

"You called me."

The counselor stopped bouncing her fingers and interlaced them into a single fist. "What do you know about all the flyers around the school today?"

"They're pretty?" Sheridan lifted her eyebrows. She trusted Mr. Talmadge. Besides, if he told he'd be in more trouble than her.

"Two days ago you took locker 572 without hesitation. Today, posters cover the walls, accusing kids of hurting the former owner. That couldn't be coincidence. No one else has done anything for years related to the situation with Ribbon Barber."

"Including you."

"Excuse me?" Miss Jones pulled back.

In a loud but slow voice, Sheridan leaned forward and repeated the words, "Including you."

"Is that right?" Miss Jones unlaced her fingers and crossed her arms.

"You sat back and watched a girl at this school get bullied so hard and so often she couldn't take it anymore. No one did anything. Not the students. Not the teachers. And not you."

"You have no idea what we've done." Miss Jones' lips pinched into a pucker. "You've only been here a couple of days."

"That's long enough to have some twit put a painted maxi pad on my back. And that wasn't the worse part. The teacher acted as if it was perfectly normal."

Miss Jones pressed her fingers to her temple while Sheridan continued.

"Some counselor you are. You knew what was happening and you did nothing. You sit behind that desk and collect paper. What did you ever do to help Ribbon?"

Miss Jones remained silent.

"That's what I thought." Sheridan sat back in the chair. "You've nothing to say now, just like you had nothing to say then. Instead, you decide to punish the only person who wants to defend her. Where are the idiots who tormented her every day? I'll tell you where. Sitting in their classrooms preparing their next attack. Ribbon's gone because you didn't have the guts to talk to her. In fact, no one even knows she's dead."

"A request from her parents."

"And you have no problem with that?"

"My hands are tied." Miss Jones faced Sheridan.

"So you blame Ribbon instead?"

"I don't blame Ribbon." The counselor's skin turned a blotchy pink.

"I have her journal." Sheridan stared down Miss Jones. "She names you. Yup. She complained about what was happening and you did nothing."

"What are you talking about?"

"Ribbon said you claimed those rich brats were jealous of her."

"I probably did say that. But that's not all I told her. I submitted document after document to the administration."

"Paperwork. Big deal."

"Sheridan." The counselor's soft tone irritated Sheridan. "By law I have to report abuse. The Safe Schools Improvement Act requires teachers and counselors to report bullies and this kind of thing." She lifted a green flyer.

"At least I'm trying to do something." Sheridan shifted in her seat.

"There were at least twenty reports Ribbon's

freshman year," Miss Jones continued. "After that she stopped coming to me."

"Of course she did. You weren't doing anything about it."

"Like what? Kids do things the teacher can't see and the cameras don't catch."

"Why not videotape the hallway of locker 572?"

"We did." Miss Jones tossed her hands in the air. "Someone covered the lens in black spray paint. It's too expensive to replace."

"Then give Ribbon a locker in the front of the building."

"Ribbon refused to move."

"Why?"

"I don't know." Miss Jones stared at the desk and pinched her bottom lip with two fingers. "Nothing I tried worked. Kids in this school won't give me names."

"Well, I will."

"Yeah." Miss Jones fanned a rainbow of flyers in her hand. "But this is not the way to do it. This is harassment. I have to report this too."

"And call my foster parents, no doubt."

"Yes." Miss Jones stood up. "But I'm willing to fight for you. I just need it in writing. Will you give me a written description of the maxi pad incident and anything else you know?"

"I've got ten pages."

Miss Jones pulled back. Her exhale was audible. She sat back down and touched a couple files on her desk. "I can't promise going public will be easy for you, but I'll promise to process it. Okay?"

"Fine." Sheridan wanted to believe the counselor, but it was hard.

Chapter 37

Ashley pushed past a tall, lanky kid in the technical drawing hallway. Once inside, she locked the door to the dark room and flipped the switch for the yellow light. She needed a place to escape, to be alone and undisturbed. Going to class was pointless. She wouldn't be able to concentrate. Her original plan was to call the DA at lunch. But she'd never make it through the slow pace of Ancient History and a lecture about the Peloponnesian Wars.

"Hello."

Ashley jumped at the voice. Beyond the curtain, a girl pulled a camera from her bag. "Get out."

"What?" The girl trembled a little but didn't move.

"I said get out of here."

"But this is my..."

"I don't care!" Ashley rushed to the table and grabbed the girl's camera. "If you don't get out of here now I'll smash this to bits."

"Okay. Okay." The trembling student reached for her camera like a mother for a hostage baby. Without putting it into the bag, the girl left, hugging her belongings to her chest.

Ashley wanted to end this phase of her life. Skipping classes and tormenting people. Not that any of it mattered. Her perfect record was as faked as Helen's French manicure. But it was hard. She imagined the teacher calling her name and there being a frantic search for her. Which was stupid. The teachers didn't do more than check a roll. Her imagination was spurred on by her guilt. The only place she deserved to be was jail. Skipping class wouldn't send her there, but hopefully the District Attorney would.

Her backpack dropped to the ground, and she slid down the black wall to the floor. The chemical smells didn't calm her as they usually did. Ashley unfolded one of the pink flyers with her name on it. At least someone got it right.

Ashley set her phone alarm to alert her at 9:00 A.M. Then she used her backpack as a pillow and curled up like a baby. A couple dozen prints hung from the line. Some of them belonged to her, abandoned on the day she discovered Ribbon's death. She closed her eyes and dozed off.

The minutes might as well have been seconds because before she could dream, her alarm beeped. The gum in her mouth was tasteless. It lacked all elasticity, yet she still worked it over with her teeth. She typed the DA's number into her phone a couple of times then erased it. What would it take to convince them? A girl was dead because of her. That should be enough.

She got up and paced the small room until she found the strength to dial the number again and pressed send. While the phone rang, Ashley kept walking. An automated menu led her through to a law clerk. The squeaky male voice on the other line said he'd connect her to one of the legal representatives. She listened to the music and wondered how many people called this line and admitted to killing someone before. The guy who answered sounded too calm. Were there so many crimes in southern California that nothing shocked people anymore?

The music stopped, and the phone on the other end started to ring. Ashley took a deep breath and then held back a scream when the phone clicked to voicemail. "You have reached the office of Carla Taylor. I can't come to the phone right now. Please leave a message and I'll return your call as soon as possible."

"For crying out loud!" Ashley hung up and strangled the phone in her fist. This was ridiculous. No wonder Ribbon gave up. Nobody cared. This shouldn't be so hard. They shouldn't ignore this. They should lock her up and melt the key. Ashley would have to find a way to get into trouble herself. Maybe she could steal a car or rob a bank.

The disappointment lasted until she heard the bell ring for the end of third period. Time for lunch and Courtney—and hell on earth. She dragged herself out of the tech center and toward the cafeteria. The clank of forks against plates blended with the raised voices of students. Ashley entered the line and nodded at the server. It didn't matter what they put on her plate, she wasn't going to eat it anyway. The gang hadn't made it to the center table yet, and it took a minute for Ashley to realize kids around her were whispering.

She set her tray on the table and glanced around. The room never drew her attention before, so it would be hard to compare today to another. But it wasn't until Courtney, Helen, and Maddie entered that Ashley could confirm her suspicions. The hush lasted as long as a blink, but it was there. The sound rose again as kids busied themselves under Courtney's gaze.

Ashley held her fork above her plate. Once Courtney's back was turned, kids stared and pointed. Maddie was the only part of the trio who seemed to notice. Courtney and Helen kept their chins poked out as if the flyers never existed.

But they did. That was unmistakable. The accusations had some effect. Ashley couldn't be sure what the final result would be. Hopefully, it meant the end of Courtney's reign. Fat chance, but Ashley could dream. Too bad Tinkerbell had a different lunch period. The true victory would happen when Courtney and the new girl came face to face. Ashley would love to see the spunky blonde tear into the queen bee.

The group crowded the table and sat down, but somehow they took up too much space.

"What's wrong with *you?*" Helen snarled.

"Don't worry, Helen." Courtney smiled. "Ashley knows this girl won't get away with it."

"Yeah." Helen leaned back. "You don't have to look so—whatever. Courtney called her dad this morning."

"The little boot-wearing hurricane that blew in will be gone by tomorrow." The leader, with the help of her father, had an amazing ability to deflect every situation.

"Personally, I'm going to miss her." Ashley straightened her back.

"Really?" Helen almost swallowed her tongue.

"Yeah." Ashley squinted up at the girl she'd wasted five years trying to impress. Ashley examined herself.

She'd become such a non-descript person. Since junior high she'd morphed into the creeps she followed. Her old friend, Ribbon, was unique. The new girl, Tinkerbell, had a sense of herself. Even Courtney had a personality that, wicked as it may be, at least belonged to her. But what did Ashley ever do to be Ashley?

Nothing.

She and Helen and Maddie were all shadows of the three-dimensional figures around them. They'd spent their high school life being vague copies of the worst girl alive.

Ashley surveyed the cafeteria. There were band geeks and science nerds and sports jocks and drama freaks. Each had been labeled based on something they *did*. They were set apart and distinctive.

"You'd better watch yourself!" Helen's threats meant nothing to Ashley. It wasn't that long ago she would have done the same thing.

"It's okay, Helen. Ashley's just joking." Courtney stared at Ashley. "Right?"

"Right." Ashley didn't turn her eyes away from her former leader. No more ducking. No more hiding. Besides, none of this high school mess mattered anymore.

"Get this out of here." Courtney pushed her tray out of the way.

Maddie jumped to her feet until Courtney lifted her hand.

"Not you. Ashley will take it."

The tray scraped across the table as Helen chuckled.

"No problem." Ashley picked it up. The police wouldn't do anything. The DA didn't even answer the phone. It was time for Ashley to take action. Ribbon wasn't around to defend anymore, but there were other kids out there. One thing Courtney needed to get straight; Ashley wasn't going to take anything from that witch again.

The eyes of all the first-lunch kids and two teachers watched as Ashley poured the entire plate of uneaten meatloaf, mashed potatoes and gravy on the meanest girl in school.

Chapter 38

I saw Ashley today.

Not the possessed girl that has been roaming the halls in her place, but the real Ashley. The one I used to know.

It was on a break between classes. That moment in the day that belongs to the bullies instead of the teachers. Normally I cringe from the bell that ends one class to the one that starts another. This time I got from English to science in seconds. Mostly because I wanted to be out of the halls as soon as possible. But also because I love the science lab. I mean, it has the skeleton of a shark hanging from the ceiling.

When I got there, Ashley had stayed late to review her paper with the science teacher. The mean girls she usually hangs out with had already left. Without them, Ashley's shoulders relaxed and her real smile appeared. I couldn't believe it, so I stood in the doorway and watched.

It was great to be invisible for that whisper of a moment.

My old friend didn't sneer at the teacher the way she did when the others were around. In fact, she laughed at something Mr. Kelly said and then scribbled his advice into her notebook. It lasted less than a minute. But she really did appear like a Charles Dickens' ghost. Then she picked up her books and came in my direction.

When she got to the hallway, I smiled. But she was gone again. Her eyes glazed over and

she pretended I wasn't there.
     I don't hate her anymore. What's the point? She's obviously as miserable as I am.

Chapter 39

Sheridan crammed her clothes into her worn suitcase. So much for adults. Miss Jones lied like the rest of them. Instead of helping fight the bullies, the counselor called the state. Not only was Sheridan suspended from school, they started her transfer to a new foster home. She would be out of San Diego before the end of the day. Forget about her overall report, it didn't matter. Let them send her back to Yuba County. One thing Sheridan was positive about, none of those evil Barbies would have to move. No. They got to keep their pathetic lives and continue to torment kids to death.

The grown-ups had no idea what it was like to be tortured day after day at school. They weren't interested in fixing what was really broken. Instead, they gave weak-kneed advice. No wonder random people rampaged supermarkets with semi-automatic weapons. It no doubt all led back to what happened to them in high school.

Miss Jones processed the transfer in less than four

hours. Sheridan shoved another shirt in the suitcase. That must be a record. San Diego was done. The empty drawer slammed closed, but then it bounced back open.

Sheridan reached over and slammed it again. It rebounded in defiance. She slapped it closed again, only to have it roll open.

"Stop it!" she screamed. With open palms, she pushed it closed and leaned against the entire dresser. The unit dented the wall. The framed picture of her and Tex crashed to the floor with a crack, followed by the ceramic lamp. "Aaaaaa," she shouted to the walls and tossed her suitcase over.

Nina didn't tap on the door but opened it firmly. Let her be mad. Sheridan had nothing to lose. They couldn't do anything more to her now except send her to jail.

The thought sobered her.

She'd gotten into trouble as a kid, but she'd never been to juvie. A couple of suspensions and warnings, but that was it. Now, her plans to stay and graduate and help avenge Ribbon were ruined.

Sheridan crumpled onto the bed.

Nina didn't shout or scold her. Instead, she said in a calm voice, "You can stop tearing up my house now." Then she bent over, unfolded the discarded suitcase, picked up the littered clothes, and began to fold them.

Sheridan moved from the bed to hide in the closet with the big box of her shoes. How do all those kids at North Harbor live with themselves? Sheridan would rather leave than ever become a sheep. She knelt on the hard surface of the closet and stacked her boots into the box. Being in high school was hard, but these kids turned it into World War III. Crazy. No matter how she tried, it didn't make sense. And now she'd be back in Yuba County without Tex, or the ability to vindicate Ribbon.

"Is there anything else I can help you with?" Nina asked.

What could this adult accomplish that all the others had failed to do?

Nina didn't look like a foster mom as she sat cross-legged on the floor beside the closet and stared out the window. "I don't know exactly what happened. I hate that you're going so soon. You must have made someone very mad. I've never had a case worker sound so rattled."

Sheridan overlapped the cardboard flaps at the top of the box and sealed it.

"As far as I'm concerned"—Nina reached into her pocket and unfolded a crumpled flyer—"you aren't the one who needs to be sorry. Sounds like you've run into some bullies that don't want to be stopped."

"You believe me?" Sheridan's voice echoed off the closet walls.

"Why shouldn't I?"

"I don't know." Sheridan picked up the box and set it by the door. "It doesn't matter anyway. It's over now."

"It doesn't have to be." Nina uncrossed her legs and set her feet on the ground. She leaned her hands over her raised knees. "These mean kids are in the minority."

"But they control the majority." Sheridan picked up the broken photo of her and Tex. The glass cracked but didn't shatter. She would replace the frame another day.

"Then remove their control."

"Excuse me?"

"Do whatever it takes to get people to stop listening to them."

"I tried. It didn't work." Sheridan put the cracked picture into the suitcase Nina had repacked and placed on the bed. She knelt down and began to pick up the shattered pieces of her small lamp. "Maybe I need to beat some sense into the creeps. Let them go through a little pain of their own."

"Bully the bullies?"

"Why not?"

"I don't know." Nina grabbed a random pair of socks. "I just wonder if it's worth becoming one of them."

The lamp was toast. Sheridan dropped the fragmented pieces into the trash. There wasn't enough glue in the world to fix it, and there was nothing in the world to fix high school.

"I think there are less aggressive solutions." Nina tucked the socks into a single ball and tossed them into the suitcase. "Like the fliers you created. That was a great idea."

"Yeah, real great. Got me expelled and kicked out of your house." Sheridan plucked tiny pieces of ceramic from the carpet, cradling them in her palm.

"Passive resistance caused Ghandi to starve and cost Martin Luther King his life."

"That was different. Nobody else wants to join the cause. Kids today won't risk danger for the sake of good. Nobody wants to talk about it.

"Everybody's scared. Honestly, I'm sick of the whole thing, including the teachers and counselors who could actually make a difference."

"In my experience, and I've had eight teenaged foster kids"—Nina tossed another ball of socks like a free-throw into the suitcase—"young people don't like to tell adults their problems. But what about to each other? If all the kids at North Harbor would get together, the handful of out-of-control instigators could be stopped."

"Look, the jocks aren't going to talk to the goths. The goths won't talk to the cheerleaders. The cheerleaders don't talk to the eggheads." Sheridan sunk to the floor across from Nina. The fatigue of the day and her late night stole all of her fight.

Nina shrugged. "Maybe you can find a way to get them together without having them talk. I don't know." She dusted fake dirt off her knee. "Do you mind if I change the subject?"

"No." Sheridan picked at the hem of her jeans.

"After you graduate, Joe and I would like for you to come back and stay with us."

"I'll be eighteen in February." Sheridan stood up.

"We know."

"The state won't provide anymore babysitting money." She grabbed a handful of clothes on hangers and dragged them over to the bed.

"It's not about the money."

"Since when is it not about the money with you?" Sheridan didn't suppress her laugh. "You have a room dedicated to every dime."

"I monitor money so I can better spend it."

"What's the catch?" Sheridan dropped the clothes on the bed.

"No catch. We believe you deserve to go to college."

"You're going to pay my tuition?"

"No."

"The catch." Sheridan slipped a shirt off a hanger and put it into her suitcase.

"We aren't offering to pay. When I went to college, my parents couldn't afford tuition. I worked nights in a doughnut shop and took out student loans. It took ten years to pay everything back. But that's beside the point." Nina shook her head. "When I was in school, students who had a full ride spent the majority of their days at the beach with surfboards. People appreciate what they earn."

"So, you'll make me work."

"You'll want to work. Joe and I will give you a place to live and food to eat, as long as you continue to go to class and get good grades. We'll even help with book fees. You'll do the rest. There are grants and scholarships. If you applied for enough, you might not even have to work." Nina stood. "Anyway. When you're up in Yuba County, think about it." She patted Sheridan on the shoulder. "I've got to fix dinner."

"Sure." Sheridan closed her eyes. This was all too much, a chance for college without having to spend all her doll-head savings on rent. She pushed the unfolded clothes out her way and fell back on the bed. She stared at the ceiling as if the decorative brush strokes could speak to her.

Chapter 40

Ashley's Dad barked, "Suspended! Are you kidding me? Mashed potatoes? Meatloaf? You don't dump food on people, especially not a Manchester. Courtney's dad is a powerful man. I should never get a call from him about something like this. You must have lost your mind. What would make you do something so stupid? This is going to impact your ..."

"Is he going to fire you?"

"Fire me? Why would he fire me over this? That's ridiculous."

"Never mind."

"Don't change the subject."

Dad's tirade continued, but Ashley stopped listening. No point in answering either. He wasn't going to hear her side anyway. It was all such a joke. No wonder the world sat on a tipped axis. The imbalance of justice must weigh it down. This escape from North Harbor High wouldn't relieve Ashley's guilt, but it was better than watching Courtney's smug face. Let Dad lock her in her room. None of it mattered.

When the lecture ended, Ashley nodded and left the kitchen. She'd deal with it. In her bedroom, she leaned against the closed door. This wasn't the jail she had planned, what with a pillow-top mattress and plush down comforter. She did have a warden. Dad worked from home ninety percent of the time. As a senior software engineer, his office space was downstairs. Right next to the front door. For some kids, a one-week suspension from school meant a vacation. This lockdown was real, even if the punishment wasn't enough. Ashley had no regret for what she'd done to Courtney. Ribbon's death demanded even more.

Her homework waited on the desk next to her laptop. Another luxury she didn't deserve. From her window, the ocean sparkled on the other side of her Point Loma neighborhood. Navy ships sliced the open water. Ashley closed the blinds and crawled into her closet and shut the door.

The darkness embraced her as clothing stroked her face. A shoe poked into her butt and she moved it out of the way. This was better. This was more appropriate for a killer. A dungeon. A never-ending pit would be even better. The world didn't make sense. The bad kids got away with murder while an amazing person died. It wasn't fair. By all things right, Ashley should be sitting in a dark cell, not confined to a closet she chose for herself.

The bedroom door opened, and Dad's voice sounded muffled through the closet walls. "Ashley, I'm sorry I didn't..." The words ended. His footsteps crossed the carpet in soft thuds. "Hello?" He dropped an expletive before she heard the door slam closed.

Whatever. Let him think what he wanted. Maybe

he'd get mad enough to send her to bad-kid boot camp. She nestled her head against the wall and embraced the thought. That would be awesome. She wanted to sleep on the hard ground and eat bugs.

A memory formed in her head, an event from the elementary school playground with Ribbon. Back then, the girl wasn't afraid of anything. When creepy Lee Dorkens challenged her to eat a spider, Ribbon got the best of him by chasing the boy around school with the live arachnid climbing her arm. Lee was a poser. He turned out to be more afraid of bugs than any other kid in school. Maybe that's why he challenged so many kids to eat them.

The thought of eight, slow-creeping, disjointed legs triggered goose bumps across Ashley's skin. She opened the closet door and rubbed her arms for good measure. As she crawled from the closet on all fours, she spotted her old "treasure" box behind a stack of *Vogue* magazines under the bed. The round hatbox would have memories of Ribbon inside.

Her door banged opened. "Ashley! Where were you?"

"In the closet." She didn't hold back the sarcasm.

"I just finished searching the house and yard for you. Why didn't you say something when I called?"

"You didn't give me time." Ashley rolled from her hands and knees into a sitting position at his feet.

"What were you doing in the closet?"

"Cleaning."

"Well." He couldn't really complain about that, now could he? After a heavy exhale, he didn't repeat the apology she heard in the closet. Instead he said, "Lunch will be ready in an hour."

"You don't have to babysit me, you know."

"Really?" He glared at her for a few seconds before he marched back out the door. Ashley stretched across the floor and shoved the magazines out of the way. She couldn't remember the last time she'd opened this box. With her back against the bed, Ashley dumped the contents onto the floor.

A rock.

A friendship bracelet.

Some plastic Happy Meal toys.

Of the dozen additional items, a sealed envelope caught her attention.

Ashley fingered the small, white rectangle with "DO NOT OPEN UNTIL YOU ARE 25 YEARS OLD." It had been a third grade assignment. Miss Anderson wanted them to practice cursive while she taught a lesson on time capsules. The exercise: "Write a letter to your future self. Then seal it, date it, and keep it somewhere safe."

Back then, she and Ribbon believed their friendship would last forever. After class they exchanged envelopes. The letter in Ashley's hand wasn't hers. It was Ribbon's.

Ashley had no idea what she'd written so long ago. No doubt her letter was tucked somewhere safely in Ribbon's things. Not that it mattered. Ashley didn't want to see how far she'd wandered from the person she was at eight.

Ribbon would never be twenty-five. Time had stopped for her. Ashley had not made one good decision since junior high. Each choice led her nowhere. She wanted more than anything to go somewhere. Too late. Ashley slipped her finger under the seal and tore open the page. She craved the wisdom of her eight-year-old best friend.

Chapter 41

DEAR FUTURE RIBBON,

Nice to meet you. I hope you're like my mom and dad, people who save the planet. Hopefully the hole in the ozone has been fixed. That way they can take a break. I'm the luckiest girl in the world to live in a place where things get to grow.

Do you and Ashley still play in the park? I hope you still remember our secret place behind the bush. No one ever found us when we went there. You're probably too big now.

At this age I like rocks. I have all sizes and colors.

Did you ever travel to New Zealand or learn to speak Chinese?

After you read this, give Ashley a huge squeeze. She's very special. Bestest friend ever. Pick Mom and Dad a bunch of daisies. And give them a big smooch.

Love from YOU, at eight years old

Chapter 42

Ribbon's letter floated to the floor. Ashley wiped her nose and face with the back of her hand. Just how much had she stolen from the Barbers? Forget about high school proms. These people lost grandchildren because of her. Mr. Barber was right. The unthinking gang threw a bunch of trash at an innocent girl. Their pollution could never be cleaned up.

The weight of Ribbon's words pressed against her heart. She put both palms to her chest and swallowed, gasping for breath. This was too much.

Ribbon should be here, alive.

Ashley should be gone.

She grabbed her knees and rocked back and forth. Each of Ribbon's words had stung, especially the idea of them lying flat on a piece of paper unread by a future self. Ashley's muscles tightened. It wasn't fair, any of it. No one deserved to be ganged up on the way they targeted Ribbon. How many days did Ribbon ache like this?

Too many.

And mostly because of Ashley's weakness. The beating

in the church the other night was nothing compared with this stabbing pain.

That's what killed Ribbon—the inexhaustible, piercing sorrow of words flung at her like stones at a leper. Ashley breathed and allowed her thoughts to settle. She'd done it, picked up rocks of hate and flung them at an innocent girl. The thought of it cut across her nerves like a rusty nail file.

Ashley wanted to end the heartache. It would be unbearable to feel this kind of sadness every day. Ashley put her face on the floor. She studied her trinkets from her sideways position.

The small items appeared large, larger than normal, while the big things like the bed and the desk were distant and far. Ribbon's letter lay like a folded tunnel shrinking the world. Ashley couldn't bring her friend back, but she could grant the girl's third-grade wish.

The room spun when Ashley sat up. She waited until the blood began to flow back into her brain. Mr. and Mrs. Barber needed to know they were not to blame. They needed to know Ribbon loved and adored them. High-school life had attacked and changed her. The daily pain of rejection drove her decision to die. Ashley chewed on the idea for a moment. Mr. Barber would never believe her, but he would have to believe Ribbon.

Until today, Ashley thought suicide happened because of selfishness or revenge. But Ribbon wouldn't have done it for those reasons. Ashley believed with everything inside her Ribbon wanted to live, but she just didn't want to hurt anymore. Her bruised heart never had a chance to heal.

Sticks and stones will break your bones. But bones will recover and mend. Words, on the other hand, leave scalding scars that fester and bleed where no one can see them.

Ashley folded the letter and slipped it back into the envelope. Her next step was obvious, even if it meant another shout-fest with Mr. Barber.

One at a time, Ashley returned her childhood mementos to the hatbox and slid it under the bed. She needed to sneak out and go to Ribbon's house. The note belonged to the Barbers.

Dad wasn't going to be happy. Ashley imagined him searching in the closet and under the bed as she crawled out the window.

Chapter 43

The social worker arrived at Nina and Joe's a few minutes before two. Sheridan and Nina carried the two suitcases and three small boxes to the car. One of the boxes wouldn't fit in the trunk.

"You have to sit in the back," the DCFS lady said. Her face was pinched in a scowl as she pushed the box across the seat to give Sheridan room.

"That's okay." No sense pretending this was anything more than a taxi ride. Sheridan turned to say good-bye to Nina and found herself yanked into an awkward hug.

"Think about what I said," Nina whispered then embraced her a little tighter.

Sheridan returned the squeeze.

Nina pulled away. "Call me and let me know you got there safely." She then reached into her pocket and handed Sheridan the cell phone she'd left on the dresser.

"Excuse me, ma'am," the tight-faced social worker said, "You can't do that."

"Do what?" Nina's eyes flashed. Sheridan stepped

out of the way.

"You can't give her that phone."

"Says who?"

"The state." The social worker laid her hand flat in the air toward Sheridan. "Since the child won't be living in your home, you won't be able to monitor the minutes or control the charges."

"Don't talk to me like I'm a child who can't add." Nina wasn't backing down. Sheridan stood stunned.

"The state won't take the liability."

"Who's asking them to?"

"Give me the phone." The worker turned her eyes to Sheridan. A moment of authority and control. Before Sheridan could react, Nina stepped between her and the social worker.

"What's your name?"

"Excuse me?"

"Your name." Sheridan peeked around Nina while the lady took a step back. "This child, as you call her, has been through enough. You're taking her back up north, and that's your job. But that's the extent of it. Now give me your name."

"Joan Willis." The lady tugged at the end of her shirt and stiffened her back. "But what does that have to do with the situation? She can't keep the phone without a release."

"What a joke." Nina wasn't laughing. "I could have given her the phone in the house. Were you planning to frisk her? You don't control everything." Nina slowed down her voice and looked at the woman as if she was a delinquent adolescent. "Listen to me, Joan. When I walk into that house, I'm going to contact your supervisor to make sure I hear from this *young lady* from *that* phone when she arrives in Yuba County. If I don't, I'll file an official complaint and take it up as high in the administration as I can."

"Do whatever you want." The DCFS worker marched around to the driver's side.

"Sheridan." Nina swiveled, her eyes bright. She spoke loud enough for the social worker to hear her. "If she asks for the phone, even once, you call me immediately."

"Yes, ma'am."

The driver's side door slammed shut and the engine started without a roar. Sheridan climbed into the backseat. The car peeled out before Sheridan could even buckle her seatbelt. She turned and watched Nina from the back window until the car made a right at the end of the block.

In a few months, Sheridan would legally be considered an adult, which was something she never thought she would be proud of until now. Nina was the real deal.

The traffic through San Diego was heavy, and Sheridan scrunched down into her seat. The hard plastic of the phone felt soft against her fingers. The DCFS worker didn't bother to glance at Sheridan in the rear-view mirror. This was the best gift Sheridan had ever been given. She turned off the power to save on the battery. Nina would have slipped the charger into one of the boxes, no doubt. But Sheridan didn't want to miss making the call to Nina, nor one right after to Tex. The woman in the front seat would have to go through more than Nina if she tried to take it now.

It wasn't a moment to miss. For the first time in her life, a woman labeled "mother" defended her. And she couldn't go back to her. Not yet. In three months she'd be eighteen. In six she'd be a high school graduate. Time. That's all. For now, she would strengthen her resolve and get ready to face Mom number six. If the DCFS worker driving her through San Diego was a sign, Mom number six might end up being a six, six, six. But it no longer mattered.

Sheridan opened her purse and dropped the phone into the oversized bag right next to Ribbon's journal. Had it been worth it to give up the best family she'd known for a girl she'd never met? Especially since Ribbon was already dead? Sheridan fished out the journal. She flipped to a random page and started to read.

Chapter 44

Mom sold my favorite plaque today. The homemade paper had threads of blue and red. One of her prettiest pieces. But that's not what I enjoyed most about it. It was the bold artistic corners on the letters. Mom's calligraphy is getting better. I also love the saying by Edmund Burke, "The only thing needed for evil to prosper is for good men to do nothing."

Now it could be that I'm over-emotional. Been studying World War II and reading novels like **The Book Thief** and **The Diary of Anne Frank**. The hardest thing to do each day is listening to the bullies at North Harbor. They are no different from other haters, and high school isn't much different from Nazi Germany.

The geeks lay low, glad it's me instead of them.

The popular kids participate to remain popular.

The scholars keep their faces in their books as if their ears don't work.

Now that Mom's sold the only quote that stirred up hope in my heart, maybe I should stop hoping that someone out there is brave enough to stop doing nothing.

There's one big problem. At this point in my life, I believe Hitler and his advisors are right that if you tell a lie long enough, people will eventually believe it. Amazing, I know. In the depth of all of this high school education the only person who speaks my language is Adolf Hitler! That man was responsible for extensive genocide. The most hated name in history speaks—no, he shouts—about my existence. Maybe Mom could make me a plaque with the quote from **Mein Kampf**.

My life is nothing but a lie anyway. Come on, Mom. What's wrong? Isn't there enough borrowed dryer lint to announce the worthlessness of my life?

I accept it in all its devastating reality. The lie that Courtney and her friends started back in junior high has become true in every brain at North Harbor. I'm ugly and stupid and I deserve to die.

Chapter 45

Sheridan could hear the social worker from behind the wall.

"Isn't there anyone else?"

"No." The male voice sounded stern. "This case has been assigned to you. Now get that child to Yuba County."

"Why can't I do it in the morning?"

"Because we don't have any temporary housing for her."

"But it's a good ten-hour drive to Yuba County from here."

"You can stop in Bakersfield for the night."

"How can one child make such a mess?"

Sheridan spotted a water cooler and hurried over for a cup. She refused to let the weight of Ribbon's death, the loss of Nina, and the hatred from overworked government people push tears from her eyes. In no time she'd be eighteen with a diploma. She just needed to count.

The door to the office swung open. The pinched-face

woman glared at her. "Let's go."

With straight shoulders, Sheridan picked up her burdens and followed the witch through the building to the parking garage. She resisted the urge to shout at the lady. "None of this was my idea!"

The DCFS worker marched toward the elevators and ignored a man who waved at her. Sheridan smiled as the guy shrugged. Life was full of unspoken symbols and non-verbal communication. This woman was disliked by more than just foster kids. Sheridan could see it all over his face. The elevator wobbled them down to the parking garage. This woman shouldn't be working with people at all.

When the doors slid open, a woman smiled at Sheridan as she stepped out of their way. The heavy-set lady had a pink ribbon pinned to her jacket.

Breast cancer awareness.

Sheridan's second foster mother wore one all the time. The pink symbol spoke without words to women who were survivors, as well as anyone else who wanted to join the fight. Tee-shirts and bumper stickers spoke without words the common belief in a cure for breast cancer. In fact, there were tons of different people who tied different colored ribbons to their shirts for various causes.

Ribbon needed a ribbon.

Sheridan stopped.

That's the answer.

"Come on."

Sheridan skipped a couple of steps to catch up. The social worker stomped to the car. Let her be mad. In her new school, surrounded by new students, Sheridan would tell Ribbon's story and recruit kids to wear ribbons to stop bullies. Even if she had to run over a couple of teachers or counselors to do it.

She would be like the kid in that pay-it-forward movie. She was tired of life telling her where to go and what to do. Her senior year would end on a high note, one filled with a cause. The "Remember Ribbon Campaign." Wow. That had a nice ring.

While her guard unlocked the car, Sheridan began a text conversation with Tex. They were only twenty miles outside of San Diego County when Sheridan discovered something about her adopted brother she never knew before. It started with a simple question:

"Would Ribbon choose suicide?"

"Lots a kids do." The illuminated message from Tex was lame. What kind of answer was that?

"Yeah, crazy ones."

"It's not 'bout being crazy."

"Then what?" Sheridan wanted to know. She'd been through mess after mess since before she started kindergarten, and she'd never thought about it for very long. The phone in her hand started playing Tex's achy-breaky ringtone. The DCFS worker in the front of the car growled under her breath.

"Hello." Sheridan kept her voice low. Not because of the grumpy woman behind the wheel, but because the conversation was private.

"Howdy," Tex drawled into the phone before he dropped the biggest bomb on her. "Sheridan, there's something I never told ya. But when I first moved to the farm, I thought 'bout it. I mean seriously thought 'bout ending it all."

"What?" That was impossible. Tex couldn't be talking about killing himself. He was the sanest person she knew.

"I didn't grow up in foster care like you."

"You make that sound like a bad thing." Sheridan slumped down in her seat.

"It was. I knew my biological ma. I loved her. When her new husband came along and decided I was too much trouble, she got rid of me. There was no greater hell than that for me."

"That sucks." She twisted one of her shoelaces. "But why didn't you tell me?"

"I was embarrassed. I didn't want to lose ya. Yer the only real family I got."

"Tex, you can never lose me."

"I know that now." His voice was confident. Reassuring. But it didn't make Sheridan feel any better. How many other people in her life seriously thought of ending it all? The thought of Tex or Elsie or any other former foster brother or sister hurting so much they wanted to end it all made her cringe. If only Ribbon had told someone.

"Promise me if you ever have those thoughts again, we'll talk about it."

Chapter 46

Ashley crept past the house and into the yard. Her pulse refused to creep. She focused on her feet. Running would draw more attention than tiptoeing the ten yards along the fence to the sidewalk and around the corner. With each step, she resisted the urge to look toward Dad's window.

If he caught her, she'd be stuck in his office on the leather time-out chair he used when she was ten. No doubt she'd be serving that sentence when she returned. But that wouldn't matter once this errand was complete.

Her car watched from the driveway. She couldn't take that for sure. Besides, the walk to Ribbon's would give her time to think about what she could say to Professor Barber. The last time was a bust. This time she had to make sure he understood how much Ribbon loved him.

One more step took her around the fence and out of Dad's line of sight. She blew a breath. The sound of traffic made it to her ears and she realized the world hadn't stopped in her anxiety. Her stomach troubled her. The upcoming confrontation twisted her gut. Ashley preferred to avoid drama. That was what had started this whole thing. If she'd ever been brave enough to stand up to Courtney, this whole thing would have turned out differently.

She patted the back pocket of her jeans. Ribbon's letter hadn't moved.

A car stopped at the crosswalk, and Ashley ran to the other side. It might be possible to leave the letter in the mailbox or in the screen door. She slowed her legs. The sidewalk wove its way through the small neighborhood streets. The old short-cut had too many memories. The indirect route would be better.

A light breeze stirred the leaves on the tall palms. Ashley puffed out a breath and shook her head. None of this should have happened. On the corner near the grocery store, a Mexican vendor sold bunches of prepackaged flowers. Roses. Carnations. Sunflowers. Daisies. The tarp above the seller snapped in the wind.

A bouquet for Ribbon's parents might make the conversation easier. Ashley reached into her front pocket. "Please be there," she whispered. But, no, the ten-dollar bill she had must be in her other jeans. She'd left the house without her purse.

The short Latina studied her as she approached. "You want to buy flowers?"

"Yes." Ashley patted her legs. "But I don't have any money."

"No money. No flowers." The woman went back to snipping stems.

Ashley searched the surrounding area for another idea. Going back home was out. Dad was probably already searching for her. Stupid. If she had waited until after lunch, he would have left her alone a couple of hours for sure. She was stuck. The idea of going further without the white-petal gift was impossible. The daisies were a must. She couldn't deliver the letter without Ribbon's eight-year-old request.

"*Señora,*" Ashley started.

"*Si.*" The lady's face didn't change.

"I have a friend. She died and I need to take her family some flowers."

"You should bring money."

"I know." Ashley constricted her forehead. "I know." She patted her pockets again and dug her fingers inside. "It's just that I wasn't thinking too clearly when I left home."

"You should think."

"Yes, yes, I know." Ashley didn't want to feel impatient. She touched her watch. That's it. Certainly the lady would barter a small bouquet of daisies for the timepiece. "How about a trade?"

"Trade?" The vendor leaned on one foot with a hand on her hip. "What you want to trade?"

"This." Ashley unclasped her watch.

"No, no. I don't need no watch." The lady shook her head.

"Please." The leather band dangled in the air.

"No. I don't need."

Ashley dropped her hands to her side. This was pointless. She re-strapped the watch to her wrist and turned to walk away when the vendor grabbed her arm.

"You said trade. I trade."

"You'll take the watch."

"No, no. I don't need no watch."

"Then what?"

"That. I trade flowers for that." The woman pointed at the ring on her pinkie finger. The small pearl Ashley felt embarrassed about after seeing Courtney's new emerald.

"No way."

"No ring. No flowers." Thick scissors snipped another crooked stem.

This was absurd. Ashley walked away. The vendor wanted to rip her off. The loud blare of a horn prevented her from stepping into the street. Wasn't this a four-way stop? A glance right and left revealed only two stop signs. She paced up the street away from Ribbon's house and twirled the ring on her finger with her thumb.

A memorial to Ribbon, that's all she wanted to do, not sacrifice her aunt's gift. The pearl didn't sparkle like a diamond or emerald. The majority of it's worth was sentimental. The small stone once made her feel like she was in a class with Courtney. Of course it never competed with expensive gems. But it was real.

Ashley leaned against a tree. The uneven rings on the palm tree's trunk dug into her back, but that didn't matter. She was a fraud. Ribbon was dead. The girl deserved the best. If her old friend were alive Ashley would give her the ring in a heartbeat. But the crafty flower vendor would probably only pawn it. Ashley pulled the ring from her finger. Maybe she could ask the vendor to hold on to the pawn ticket, and Ashley could buy back the ring herself. That's it. She'd buy the flowers and recover the ring. The price would be higher than she'd planned, but what's the big deal? If she had fifty bucks in her pocket she'd spend it all on flowers. The temporary loss of the ring wouldn't cost her more than that.

She closed her palm around the ring and headed back to the vendor.

"You've got a deal." Ashley extended her open hand.

The woman pinched the ring between two fingers and held it up to the light as if she suddenly questioned its value. With a nod, the woman pocketed the ring and grabbed the largest bouquet of roses from an orange bucket.

"Nope." Ashley pointed to the small bundle of daisies. "I want those."

"No, no. Those very cheap. These more expensive."

"I know. But daisies were my friend's favorite." Ashley selected a batch for herself. Water dripped from their stems onto the hot concrete.

"Okay." The vendor shrugged. "You choose." The lady took the flowers and wrapped the stems in a wet paper towel she secured with a rubber band.

"Thanks." Ashley took the bunch and inhaled. The weed-like smell reminded her of clean bed sheets. The sweet scent of roses had always been Ashley's favorite. But daisies fit Ribbon.

"Oh, yeah." Ashley remembered her plan. She swung back toward the vendor. "Please. Are you here every day?"

"No. I change places sometimes. But I'm here for this month."

"Great. About the ring. Keep the pawn ticket. I'll come back and buy it from you."

"¿Qué?"

"The ring. When you sell it, save the pawn stub. I'll come back later and give you fifty dollars for the ticket." That meant Ashley would have to sneak out again. Dad would probably build a moat. But that was a problem for another day.

"Sorry. I no sell ring."

"Excuse me?"

"I no sell ring. Ring for my daughter, in Mexico."

Ashley's arms dropped to her sides, and a couple petals floated to the sidewalk. She never guessed. That wasn't part of her plan. Should she demand the ring back? She lifted the flowers to her chest. The small daisy petals quivered in the wind. What did it matter? If the DA or police ever got a clue, the ring would be confiscated anyway. The gift in her hand was worth more than bent metal.

Chapter 47

Sheridan was probably seven years old the last time she looked forward to meeting a foster parent. But the twenty-four-hour commute with Cruella Deville would have that effect on anyone. Ribbon's journal never mentioned the quote, "If you can't beat them, join them," but Sheridan was ready to make the best of the next few months. Give her the tee-shirt, she'd join the club. Besides, when February 15 came around, she would become a part of the crowd she hated so much. Grown-ups.

As the car brakes squealed to a stop in Marysville, Sheridan texted Nina of her safe arrival. She'd never lived in this particular part of Yuba County, but she'd been here. The fresh air comforted more than her lungs. It smelled familiar.

"Are you Sheridan? Of course you are. I don't see any other young people around." An elderly lady leaned against an old car. "Come on over here, dear."

Sheridan put her cell phone in her purse and watched the social worker peel out of the Marysville

Greyhound station.

"I know what you're thinking. I'm way too old to be a foster mother. Ha ha. You're probably right. But I have the credentials. Yes, I do. I can tell you that. Before my wonderful husband, Joyce, died, we had taken in over one hundred kids. Yes, that's more than a century's worth of young people. I guess in this generation Joyce is a strange name for a man. Lots of teasing with a name like that, you bet. But he wasn't the only man named Joyce in the world. Maybe you've heard of the poet who wrote about trees. He went by Joyce too. Lots of teasing with a name like that, you bet."

A couple of men clomped toward them in cowboy boots. One tipped his John Deere baseball cap before picking up Sheridan's suitcases. The other didn't make eye contact at all while he put her boxes into the back of their pick-up truck.

"Don't worry about them. Those are some of my boys. I have tons of them around. They always help out an old lady like me. One thing about kids, if you treat them nice when they're little, they'll treat you nice when you get old. There's plenty of people around to help me when I need it. Something for you to remember if you think you want to be one of those kids who likes to beat-up on old ladies." She paused. "You one of those kind of kids?" Her painted-on eyebrows lifted halfway up her forehead.

"No, ma'am."

"Good, I didn't think so. It never hurts to ask, but big trouble can come if you don't ask." She squeezed Sheridan's face with a boney hand. "You have a nice look. Reminds me a bit of a fairy or something. I don't mean a gay person. I mean like a flying magical fairy. Sorry. I'm just old enough now to let whatever I want fall out of my mouth."

The grown men she called boys waved bye to Sheridan's new foster-care provider. The doors to the pick-up slammed shut before the truck coughed away.

"It's nice, you know, to be free to speak my mind. Not enough of that these days, what with texting and stuff. Shoot, people don't hardly talk at all anymore. By the way, my name's Miss Shirley. All my kids call me Ma Shirley, but you can start off with Miss if that's more comfortable to you. Gotta be hard to change moms as if they're clothes or something. A mom's supposed to fit for life."

The lady stepped over to her car, adjusted her wig, and got behind the big steering wheel. The passenger door was heavy as Sheridan opened it in a wide arc. She sat on the long, undivided front seat and pulled the old-fashioned seatbelt across her waist. The car was too old to have a shoulder strap, let alone air bags. The interior smelled like lotion. One thing was for sure. The last few months of her foster-child life wouldn't be quiet. Thank goodness she had a plan to fill her school days. She'd just spent the long commute texting with Tex about the new "Remember Ribbon Campaign." The purpose was to get kids to stop bullies without risk. Get them to talk without talking. It would be interesting to conduct that plan while living with someone who blabbed on and on without saying anything important.

"You all buckled, darlin'? Great. I might as well tell you now as ever, I don't like any distractions while I'm driving. I'm an old lady and I need to focus. My driving record is clean as a whistle and I want it to stay that way. You understand?" Miss Shirley smiled. "That means no radio or conversation. I know that bothers some kids. Others adjust just fine. All my attention needs to be on the road."

"Okay."

Miss Shirley leaned forward over the steering wheel and inched the antique vehicle onto the road. Sheridan cranked down her window and let the cool northern air wisp into the car. No need to worry. It would be hard to die in a car traveling twenty-five miles per hour. They passed a city park, and Sheridan was able to count every tree. By the time they crossed a couple of bridges, she leaned her head on the back of the seat and closed her eyes.

The best way to kick off the campaign would be to tell Ribbon's story. She and Tex had it all worked out. She'd find a teacher or counselor or some other older person who would listen. This time she would be calm and persuasive and present it as a social experiment. The idea would be to get the kids to band together with people they didn't even know to stop bullies. Then she would explain about the ribbons. It was Tex's idea to avoid a single color. Especially because guys wouldn't get into it if they had to fold and pin something to their clothes. Instead, they decided the type of ribbon didn't matter; the color, pattern, size or style of ribbon. Kids like to be unique. The message had to be subtle enough to avoid becoming targets. Girls could wear a green one in their hair. Boys could loop a black one through a zipper on their backpack. They could be used as shoe laces or key chains. Kids could tie them around their wrists or hang them from the rings of spiral notebooks.

Sheridan opened her eyes and squinted at the brightness of the day. They'd left the town. Cows chewed grass in pastures around her. She had spent the majority of her life in the country, with no memories of the mother who abandoned her to a drug addiction. Her birth certificate listed her father as "unknown." Rejection became something she accepted, until she made a brother of Tex.

The heavy smell of manure overtook the clean rural air. Of course, she'd forgotten about that. Her nose would adjust. The endearing driver hunched over the wheel in deep concentration. Tomorrow, Sheridan would go to school and start her ribbon campaign. Life might just work out.

Chapter 48

Ashley scratched the pinkie finger on her right hand. Her finger missed the ring. The Barber's house loomed less than fifty steps away. Ashley slowed her pace. She attached Ribbon's letter to the stem of a daisy with a safety pin she found on her belt hoop.

There was no need for conversation or confrontation. Professor Barber didn't have to be bothered. Mrs. Barber could stop defending her. They could find the note and curse Ashley for eternity.

The overgrown yard waved at her in the breeze. She accepted its invitation and hurried the last ten steps to the porch. This would all be over soon. A seagull squawked across the sky, and Ashley carefully ascended the first couple of steps. Before she reached the top, she stretched her arm and the bouquet toward the door. The love-me-love-me-not bunch rested against the screen, and the envelope flapped in the breeze.

That's it.

Ashley turned to tiptoe down the steps and almost bumped right into Mrs. Barber.

"My goodness, what are you doing here?"

"Um." Heat rose up Ashley's neck to her face. "I wanted to leave you something." She pointed to the porch. "Ribbon's favorite flower."

"Oh, that's so sweet." Mrs. Barber's steps weren't heavy as she climbed the steps and rescued the abandoned bouquet. "They're such a peaceful flower."

Ashley rubbed the free space on her pinkie finger. "She brought me a handful of them in the third grade when she heard my bird had died."

"Sounds like her." The woman fingered the envelope. "What's this?"

"A letter from Ribbon."

"What?" Mrs. Barber froze.

"From the third grade," Ashley hurried to tell her.

"Oh." The woman took a moment to thaw. When she finally moved, she undipped the safety pin and tucked the letter into her large apron pocket. "Come on, let's put these in some water."

Mrs. Barber took the stone path toward the backyard. Ashley had been in the garden once in fifth grade. They grew the most delicious corn and watermelons in the world. Ashley didn't want to run off, but she wanted to stay even less. Ribbon's mother stopped at the shed. She laid the flowers on a weather-beaten table. "Fill this from the tap, will you?

Ashley took the extended Mason jar, glad to have some activity. It felt like eyes watched her from Ribbon's bedroom, but Ashley kept her gaze front and center. While it would have been more than creepy to see Ribbon watching from the window, it would have been beyond terrible to look into the professor's face.

"Thank you, dear." Mrs. Barber gently separated the daisy stems. "Do you mind staying around and helping me a little? I took a leave from teaching for a while. This neglected yard might take an army to fix it up."

"I'm not supposed to be here."

"Why not?"

"I'm suspended from school."

"Then I'd say you have the time." Her voice was perfectly natural as she spoke. Her face showed no indication that it would be odd to have her dead daughter's friend help her do yard work. Of course, in any other circumstance, it would be normal. People helped grieving people all the time.

"My father thinks I'm at home. Grounded in my room."

"Well, I'll fix that." She patted Ashley's arm. The backdoor screen bounced a couple times as Ribbon's mother disappeared into the house. The sun stared at her and the whole day was too bright for her eyes.

Her cell phone hummed. Probably her dad calling to cuss her out about leaving the house and bothering the Barbers. Ashley took a peek at the screen. It was a text message. She regretted it as soon as she opened the phone.

"Tell your dad to kiss his job good-bye," Courtney's message threatened.

Great. Unemployment would certainly trump her suspension. Ashley didn't like that Dad would reject Mrs. Barber. But the quiet, soft hum of bugs in the yard and the gentle sway of unpulled weeds whispered pity to her soul. She was getting what she'd earned.

Ashley turned and faced the chain link fence covered in wild grapes. It was ridiculous for her to get upset earlier when the vendor wanted her ring. She needed to go home and empty her room of every kindness ever given to her. But that wasn't going to happen.

"Your father said he'd pick you up at 5:00 P.M."

Chapter 49

Sheridan's room smelled like dust. But it was clean and the bed was made. Large stacks of books and magazines lined the walls. Miss Shirley had turned an old bedroom into a library, and now back into a bedroom. It was a transition home.

Whatever. It was only for a few months. And Nina's offer started to sparkle. A few months of moths and cobwebs weren't that scary.

"Okay. How are you set?" Miss Shirley leaned her weight on the door knob as she stood. "Sorry about the room, but it's just for a bit. You'll be up and outta here in no time. Now, I figure you're hungry so I made some soup. I'm not much of a cook, never was. Thank the good Lord for crockpots. Joyce fixed all the meals for most of our marriage. He or the kids helped. Did I tell you it was over one hundred? Yup, those kids taught me more about cooking than anyone else. So, if you have some kitchen skills, that would be great. You tell me what you want and I'll make sure one of the boys picks up the ingredients from the store."

"Thanks." It was the only word Sheridan could squeeze in.

"Now as for school, I'm not much for the public education system. Seems like there's just too much trouble these days. I'm not much for a teacher taking a switch to a student. Nope. Met too many mean teachers when I was a kid who seemed to do it just for fun. But, these kids nowadays need a lot more discipline then they get. So, I like to keep 'em right where I can see 'em."

Up until now, Sheridan didn't have a problem understanding what the old lady said. "Are you saying I won't be going to school?"

"Not to the public school."

"Then how will I graduate?" The words hurried from Sheridan's mouth before Miss Shirley could say something else.

"It's called homeschool, honey. All my children have been homeschooled, and they are out in the world doing just fine. Don't you worry. I'm an accredited teacher and have been approved by the state. It took a few years and a lot of fight to get the approval, but I've had it for a number of years. We'll make sure you finish all the classes you need right in that schoolhouse over there." She pointed a gnarled finger toward the window. A big red barn stood fifty feet beyond the fence. "And we'll submit your work through a state approved school."

"You mean I'm not going to be with other people my age?"

"Not exactly. We meet each month with the other homeschoolers for field trips, and sometimes will join the public schools in spelling bees and such." Miss Shirley sat in the swivel chair at the desk.

No way. She couldn't do the Remember Ribbon

Campaign from a shed. Man, the entire universe was against her. If she wasn't in the school system, how was she ever going to make a difference? All her life she wanted to escape the chaos, and now she had a purpose, she'd be stuck in a room made for cows and playing school with a talkaholic old lady. She couldn't catch a break.

"Honey, don't scowl like that, you'll get wrinkles. You don't want to look like me when you get old, now do you? Seems to me school hasn't been the best place for you. This will be a chance to finish your classes without any of the *drama*, as my girls put it. You're not the first who didn't like the idea, but my other kids got used to it. In the end I think you'll like it."

"You were saying something about food?" Sheridan was ready to swallow swill to get her out of listening to any more bad news.

"Oh my, yes." Miss Shirley stood up. "Of course. That's what you need, a good, old-fashioned bowl of Minestrone soup. It's been simmering all day. I'll go in and set the table while you freshen up. I think after we eat, we can both settle down for a nice little rest. Naps don't have to be wasted on babies you know. They can be very refreshing."

"Yes, ma'am," Sheridan answered. She might as well be back in kindergarten. Preschool in Old MacDonald's barn—afternoon naps and long, boring stories.

Chapter 50

Today is my birthday and I'm 15. I'm not even sure why I'm still alive.

I've been writing suicide plans for over a year. Guess I'm too chicken to go through with it.

Mom made me a cake.

A couple of years ago it would have been hard not to eat a second or third slice. This year I didn't even finish the first one. I wore my pretend smile and thanked Dad for the ulexite stone. The rock was more transparent than I could ever be.

I don't like to feel lonely when I'm surrounded by people. But it seems when my family gets together my isolation doubles. The weeks leading up to my birthday have been very low. The emptiness in me grows like Mom's garden. I'm tired in more places than my mind. At my age I should be running around instead of being jealous of senior citizens.

I should have just killed myself when I first thought about it. My life hasn't gotten any better. Some days it dresses up and pretends to be something sweet and worthwhile. But it never lasts. The deep pain in my chest comes back harder after the happy days. So I just try to avoid anything that tricks me into thinking it will be alright.

Don't think for one moment that I control it. The emotions come and go as they like. When I least expect it life smacks me across the face.

I stare in the mirror so that I can hate myself more. I look at the ugly face and tell myself I'm not worth it. It's hard enough being a female high school student with all the rules about being skinny, popular, smart, and pretty. I'm a worthless dog. Get it over with already.

Chapter 51

Ashley spent every day of her suspension in Mrs. Barber's backyard.

The events of Ribbon's death came out in patches mixed with silence and tears over the few days. Professor Barber had found Ribbon's body on a noose in her closet. Mrs. Barber decided to keep the death out of the media.

"I work on a campus full of kids who are often confused and vulnerable." Mrs. Barber raked her dirty apron with her fingers. "My brother is a teacher in South Wales. Not long ago, a young girl in that area died like Ribbon."

Ashley stirred the compost heap.

Mrs. Barber sat back on her heels and stared at the fence. "Over the next two days, two more kids tried. One succeeded. Turns out the area had six other suicides. Losing my daughter was the worst thing I'll ever experience. I couldn't risk any copycats."

Sorrow rose in Ashley throat. At this moment she wished her logical mind didn't connect the dots. But her brain did the math involuntarily. Mrs. Barber held

Ribbon's death close to her chest not to protect herself or her husband. She did it to protect other kids.

Kids like Ashley.

Mrs. Barber knelt back over the garden soil and stabbed her spade into the earth. Ashley wished the sharp blade had been applied to her heart. She craved the moment she would reap what she sowed. She'd killed someone and deserved something worse than that.

Hatred.

Punishment.

She should be dragged through the streets. People should pour every disgusting thing both physical and verbal over her. Ashley glanced up at Ribbon's bedroom windows. The yellow curtains hung limp behind the glass. Her father wasn't watching today. Ashley wasn't worth the minor relief his justified hate provided her.

Ashley shoveled more compost through its phases. Worms wiggled out of the way. The weight of her part in Ribbon's death crushed her lungs. This family had a right to be left alone. It was stupid of her to want to tell the world. And it was cruel for her to want to tell these parents the extent of Ribbon's suffering. Ashley should be the one rotting under eight feet of trash and leaves.

They had a right to be spared the details. Besides, Ashley had no right to lift the mountain from her shoulders and dump it on the Barbers' memory of events. The noblest thing she could do was keep her guilt inside. Let it eat through her and decay her soul rather than unburden herself and cause this family more pain.

Better they never know. And if they found out from someone else, then she'd finally reach the kind of disgust she honestly earned. So far, she had no right to live each day camouflaged as a friend and not a fiend.

With dirt under her formerly manicured nails, Ashley grabbed the wheelbarrow and pushed it over to the maturing fertilizer. Ribbon's mom pulled weeds and watered the garden, applying organic protection against the enemies of leaves. Ashley raked through the compost and then shoveled it from one heap to the next.

The rancid smell turned her stomach. But she deserved worse. She looked up and saw Professor Barber glare at her through the screen door. He had a right to despise her. His own child should be tending the garden, not Ashley.

The back door slammed open. "Honey, there's a delivery here for you.

"Wow." Mrs. Barber dusted the dirt off her hands as the professor left the box on the back porch and went back inside. The anger from Ribbon's father was mild compared to the scalding pain of being loved by the mother.

"It's a box of flowers." Mrs. Barber opened the card and gasped. With her hand to her heart, she sat on the back step.

"Is there something wrong?"

"No. No. The flowers are for our garden. But the givers also have decided to donate fifty thousand dollars to our environmental charity in Ribbon's name."

"No way." Ashley couldn't remember the last time she'd felt happy. But something close to joy allowed her skin to notice the warm touch of the sun. The flowers spread out in an array of purples and pinks. The Barbers deserved that much and more.

Ribbon's mother fanned herself with the note.

"So who sent it?"

"Mr. Manchester and his daughter, Courtney."

Chapter 52

Sheridan's first few days of homeschool weren't horrific. The morning lessons were assigned the day before, and Miss Shirley let her do them anyplace she found comfortable. She finished her math and English assignments while playing fetch with the old lady's Weimaraner, Nancy. The gray dog would run after anything Sheridan threw.

Each day after lunch, Miss Shirley would pull out a college textbook and they'd have a lesson from it. On the fourth day, the subject was sociology. Sheridan sat with Miss Shirley in the big front yard on a bench under a naked plum tree. The foster mother had a basket of yarn she rolled into a ball. The book sat propped open on the bench between them. A paperweight made of polished stone kept the December breeze from turning the page. Miss Shirley asked, "Do you think a single person can make a difference in the world?"

"I guess." Sheridan picked up the soggy chew toy Nancy dropped at her feet and flung it across the yard. "But most people just don't care."

"What do you mean?"

"I don't know. People I've met only worry about what happens to *them*." Nancy loped back to the bench. "They don't want to get involved helping others unless they can profit from it."

"Like foster parents, you mean."

"Sure." Sheridan rubbed her hands together. Her fingerless gloves kept the slight chill from her palms. It was cool how Miss Shirley wasn't afraid to talk about the system. "But it's not only them. I'm guilty myself."

"Of what?" Miss Shirley continued to roll warm yarn.

"Being blind." Sheridan scratched the soft skin beneath Nancy's ears. "I lived in a house where a little girl was being hurt, and I never saw it. I never did anything until after it was too late."

"If you're talking about your former foster home, they told me about that." Miss Shirley focused on her growing ball of green yarn. "They wanted me to be aware of all the circumstances. I know you didn't leave Yuba County because of your behavior. And your acting out in San Diego makes me no never mind." She kept winding her yarn. "Now about that farmer, don't you go blaming yourself. Those kinda people keep their dirt hidden under deep carpets. There's no way you would have known to look."

"Maybe." The dog sat and bounced her head back and forth between Sheridan and Miss Shirley. Of course she wanted someone to pick up the rubber toy and throw it, but she made a good show of paying attention to their conversation. "I just wish I could tell Elsie I'm sorry."

"Is Elsie the little sister you had?"

"Yeah."

"Well, if that's what's troubling you, let me see what I can do. Don't see no reason why we can't arrange some kinda meeting."

"That would be nice." Sheridan patted Nancy's head. "Elsie's only one example."

"Come on, child, tell me. You know you have to trust other people sometime. Don't get me wrong. You've had a lot of evidence to the contrary, but most people are good and kind and don't like that kinda junk. It's only the bad folks who get all the attention. I've raised over a hundred foster children. And while some of them liked to stir up a beehive just to get stung, there's still some good buried in all that mischief." Miss Shirley yanked a long line of yarn from the basket. It fell into her lap and she started to roll it around the sphere.

"There's some stuff from San Diego." Sheridan picked up Nancy's squeaky chew toy and began to pluck off blades of grass.

Miss Shirley stopped her ball making. "Did someone hurt you?"

"Shoot, they'd be hurting more than me if they tried."

A heavy chuckle shook Miss Shirley's thin frame.

"It's someone else." Sheridan bounced the rubber toy on her knee, and the dog snatched it. Nancy stood for a moment with the toy clamped between her teeth before she pranced toward the barn. "A girl died by suicide because the kids at school bullied her."

"Oh. I heard about that on the news." Miss Shirley put her finished purple ball into a basket and started a new red one.

"Not this one. Everyone's keeping quiet. Usually when something like this happens it's all over the news, but I only found out about it because I inherited her locker and journal."

"How's that your fault?"

"I want to do something, but I can't 'cus I'm stuck here."

"What do you mean stuck?" Miss Shirley placed the yarn in her lap and leaned back on the bench. "We might be in the country, but we have televisions and Internet like the rest of the world. You see that pole over there? It actually brings electricity right into the house. Imagine that. Maybe next year we'll get running water."

Miss Shirley was a mess, but the best kind. Sheridan picked off small tuffs of yarn from her gloves. Why couldn't the world have more Miss Shirleys in it?

"I'm waiting. What kind of city stuff are you missing out on?"

"I want to help others." Sheridan pulled her feet up onto the bench and hugged her knees. "I have a plan to help stop bullies. I just need to be at school to do it."

"Oh, really?" Miss Shirley set the small ball on her lap, and the yarn unraveled. "Some of my children have gone on to do amazing things, I'm proud to say. And they were homeschooled." The old lady took Sheridan's hand and didn't let go. "Stop making excuses."

Sheridan wasn't comfortable holding Miss Shirley's hand, but she didn't want to yank it away. That would be rude. Instead, their fingers remained entwined in an awkward embrace. "How can I do that if the kids are there and I'm here?"

Miss Shirley's soft hand squeezed Sheridan's a little tighter. Her jaw moved as the old lady chewed on her thought. After an eternity, she released Sheridan's hand, picked up the yarn, and began to twist it over the growing ball. "What do you have in mind?"

"In the girl's journal she had a quote that said something about evil prospering because good people don't do anything. I don't want to be one of those do-nothing kinds of people. I thought if I told her story to the kids they'd get a clue."

"That's a great plan. But don't you think it's a little small? Not very earth-shattering or anything." The ball grew as Miss Shirley rotated thread after thread around it at various angles.

Sheridan fiddled with the pages of the textbook.

"Don't get me wrong. You should go to the school and speak. And there are a couple of teachers I know who might be willing to let you come to their class. But that's just a drop of water. You're trying to stop an ocean."

"Right." Sheridan didn't like the disappointment rising in her gut. "I thought about writing to the newspaper."

"I like that. We'll consider it an English assignment. Write it out tomorrow morning and I'll grade it. Then when it's good and clean we'll send it off to the local papers."

"How about I send it to some of the papers in San Diego too? I want to make the news nationwide." Sheridan swung her feet to the ground. If someone told her a couple weeks ago she'd be scheming social change with an elderly lady, she'd have called them nuts.

"Then send it to the *LA Times*. Those newspaper people love this kind of stuff. If you're willing to do that much, then I'll help you reach the rest of the world."

"What are you talking about?'

"Now, don't you worry about that. You just get to

writing. And if you do good on this newspaper business, I've got an idea that might just put you into one of those textbooks after all."

Sheridan smiled. The lady was a dreamer, that's for sure. It didn't matter what the woman had up her sleeve. Sheridan had the go-ahead to help Ribbon.

Chapter 53

R aw eggs. Ashley could smell them before she got to her locker. Let them junk it up and call her names. At least she didn't have to pretend anymore. The last thing she wanted to do was talk to the biggest hypocrite in the whole world.

Flowers. Money. As if Courtney could cover Ribbon's death with bribes.

The knob on her locker was slimy. Ashley didn't care. It served as evidence that she was out of the loop. The week spent at the Barbers provided important punishment. And Dad wanted her to go over there every Saturday until he said stop.

Good. The inside of her locker dripped with fresh milk from the door vents. Ashley grabbed her Biology book and closed the door. She'd keep it in her backpack. That's what Ribbon used to do. That wasn't the only thing Ashley would do different today.

Classes would change too. She could focus on learning instead of passing notes. Teachers would be people she'd listen to without criticism. Other kids could wear and say and think whatever they wanted. She no longer needed to have an opinion ready to present at the lunchtime council.

Ashley had released a weight so heavy the taunts and stares and ugly insinuations that came her way didn't matter. High school was temporary. If only her brain would have calculated that math problem years ago.

The slam of her locker door put an exclamation point at the end of her thoughts. Let the pushing and shoving begin. It was worth it. She'd wasted so many years in the cold shadow of Courtney. Too bad she didn't notice the darkness back in junior high.

Two kids crashed into her on the stairs. In another lifetime that would have bugged her, but today she only laughed. She was still chuckling when she passed Helen in the hall and entered the science lab.

"Ashley," the teacher's aide called her over to the front desk. "Miss Jones would like to see you in her office this morning. I'll mark you on the roll. It sounded important, so you'd better go now." The young man handed her a red hall pass.

"Okay." Ashley went back into the emptying hallway. Wouldn't it be great if her suspension had been extended? Another week from these angry halls would be fantastic. But what if it wasn't about being suspended? Courtney's father could have gone to the police.

She slogged down the stairs to the second floor. Three kids she knew of for sure got sent to juvie because of Courtney. It was one thing to go to jail for her crime against Ribbon. But it sickened her to think she'd be punished for dumping her lunch on Courtney's head.

Caroline, the student aide, looked up at Ashley from her desk. Her ever-present brown cardigan hugged her like a straitjacket. The girl had been the butt of jokes in Ashley's not-so-distant past. Now, the girl blinked at Ashley through her thick-rimmed glasses. A sweet girl with pretty blue eyes. Ashley couldn't help but smile at her.

"I'm here to see Miss Jones."

"Fine." Caroline shrugged with an I-don't-care attitude.

How many kids in this school hated Ashley? Probably the same number that hated Courtney.

"Thank you." Ashley gave the girl a genuine grin. The desire to be nice to this girl was a surprise to Ashley. The bigger shock was the soft smile the girl returned. It was kind. Of course, it didn't mean the girl liked her. It was one of those contagious smiles. Like when a kid across the room yawns, other kids start yawning too.

She headed down the narrow, internal hallway to Miss Jones' office. Ashley never really smiled at other kids before. Not even within the gang. She had no idea when a kind gesture became a weakness. The gang had lots of laughs at the expense of others. But they never smiled.

Miss Jones pointed to the overstuffed chair in her office. Ashley's nerves kicked against her gut.

"Am I still in trouble?"

"No." The bracelets on Miss Jones' wrist jingled as she waved the thought away. "I need to talk to you about something else."

"Okay." Please don't let it be about Ribbon.

"Did you know a girl named Ribbon?"

Crackers. Ashley exhaled through her nose. This was it. Courtney was going to blame the entire thing on her and get her sent to jail. Whatever. The week of suspension had been such a big relief that prison bars had to be better than high school window panes.

"Ashley?"

"Yes." She sat forward and nodded. "I knew Ribbon. She was my best friend in elementary school. I turned on her in junior high. And then I tortured her to death in high school. You probably already knew that."

"Wow." Miss Jones sat back and crossed her arms. "That's not quite what I expected you to say."

"I'm done denying it."

"Hmmm." The counselor scratched her cheek first and then the hair at the nape of her neck. "Okay. What about Sheridan?"

"Who?" Was there another kid out there who'd killed themselves? Maybe Mrs. Barber's fears about a copycat death had come true.

"Sheridan Alexander."

"Never heard of him."

"It's not a him, it's a her. She was a transfer student here for a few days, and then the administration sent her back."

"Oh. Tinkerbell."

"Excuse me?"

"Nothing." Ashley studied the cuticles on her right hand. There was no way Tinkerbell would have killed herself. Was there?

"Listen, I called you into my office today because Sheridan has contacted the *LA Times,* and a reporter was looking to corroborate her story. As a counselor, I can't speak for the events that caused Ribbon's death. But..." She leaned her elbows on her paper-crowded desk.

"No way." Ashley couldn't talk to the press.

"Why not?"

"I just can't." Ribbon had a right to rest in peace. Besides, she promised Mrs. Barber. The concerned mother had good reason to keep quiet.

"Don't you want the bullying to stop?"

"Yes." Ashley nagged the gum in her mouth. "You can think whatever you want about me, but I won't talk to the newspaper."

"The man wants to print the piece, but he can't without verifying the facts. I don't know of anyone else in this tight-lipped school who has done anything to fight back." Miss Jones' curly hair exaggerated the frustration Ashley saw on her face. "Except you. I know the mashed-potato incident was some kind of payback. But you need to find a better way to do it. And this is the way." The counselor reached over and tore a section from a yellow legal pad. "Posters and food fights don't solve anything. But if you can get the media involved, things could change."

"It doesn't matter." There was nothing Miss Jones could say. The decision wasn't hers. It belonged to the Barbers, and they'd already made their choice.

"If you change your mind, here's the phone number." Miss Jones extended her hand. Ashley crunched the folded piece of paper and stuffed it in her pocket.

"What do you know about Courtney Manchester? Seems like most of my complaints are about her. Do you have any news about her?"

"I don't have anything to say."

"That's too bad."

"Can I go now?"

"Yes."

Ashley shouldered her backpack and tromped back to class. When she got to the lab, she pulled out the yellow wad of paper and dropped it into the trash can near the door. Miss Jones better be careful, especially if she wanted to keep her job.

Chapter 54

Mom told me she almost married a plumber once. The guy wasn't a plumber at the time she dated him, but that's what he is today. Of course I know if my mother married someone other than my father then I wouldn't be here.

That's obvious. And probably not such a bad thing.

But as crazy as it sounds I wonder what it would be like to be the daughter of a plumber. For some reason I think my life would be simpler. You know, a regular kind of existence. The man would come into the house after a long day. He'd wear a work uniform and fix stuff. Not just kitchen and bathroom stuff, but life stuff.

If I wasn't Ribbon, daughter of two college professors who've spent their life dedicated to the environment, maybe my life wouldn't suck so much. Don't get me wrong. I'm glad my mother and father want to save the planet. Call me selfish if I wish someone wanted to save me.

Chapter 55

Sheridan bounced her yellow-flowered Wellies on the grass. There was no rain. She'd worn the boots because they were Elsie's favorite. A crisp wind spoke of winter while the last whispers of barbecue floated from a backyard grill. Her little foster sister came around the corner in a small baseball cap. Her straight brown ponytail poked out the back. Sheridan stood up, ready to run to the ten-year-old.

A second glance told her to stop. Elsie didn't make eye contact. Instead, she clung to the hand of her new mother. The woman crouched down so her face was even with Elsie's. Sheridan couldn't read lips, but the couple's body language spoke volumes. Why would Elsie need encouragement to see Sheridan? Whatever was said worked because Elsie came forward. Her new mother joined Miss Shirley on a bench down the park's winding path.

"Elsie, how are you?"

"Fine."

"You look nice. Is that your new mom?"

Elsie nodded and looked back at the woman for reassurance. Sheridan didn't like that Elsie only sat down after receiving a signal from the woman. But inside, satisfaction brushed across her like the rare warmth in winter. Elsie was safe.

"Have you talked to Tex since we left?"

"No." The girl twiddled her thumbs.

"Well, he says, 'hi.' I talk to him all the time."

"Oh." One small thumb passed over the other, making circle after circle.

"Elsie, are you okay?"

"Yes." The small girl made another glance toward the older women. This was more than uncomfortable. The months apart shouldn't have put this much distance between Sheridan and the girl she used to make pancakes for. But there was a wall there for sure.

"Well, I don't want to bother you. I just came to see if you are okay."

Sheridan tapped her yellow boot on the ground. One more sister lost to the system. Maybe Tex was the only sibling she'd keep from her youth. This reunion was a bust. Sheridan reminded Elsie too much of the farm. Maybe the torment the girl experienced brought back too many ugly memories. Either way, it was good to know she was secure.

"Sheri?"

"Yeah." Sheridan resisted the urge to hug Elsie at the sound of the nickname.

"Can you tell Tex something for me?"

"Of course." Sheridan squeezed her own hand to keep from grabbing Elsie's.

"No more pictures."

"No more what?"

"The pictures on the telephone poles. Can you tell him to stop?" Elsie eyes were greener than Sheridan remembered; a bright hint of spring after a long rain.

"He has stopped. He hasn't put any posters up since we left the farm."

"Good." The girl didn't look up. She continued her thumb game.

"But Elsie, he didn't do it to hurt you." The thought stabbed a hole in Sheridan's heart. Both she and Tex only wanted to punish the wicked farmer, never inflict more pain on his victim.

"I don't like it when everyone knows."

"But secrets aren't good."

"I know." Elsie brought her thumb to her mouth. She chewed on the nail. "But isn't it okay to let the grown-ups take care of it?"

Elsie's new mom sat over on the bench nodding at the endless flood of words from Miss Shirley. The words didn't make it across the windy path, but Sheridan knew they were kind. Not everyone in the system sucked. The brilliant flyer idea hurt the one person it was meant to vindicate. Sheridan had stapled as many posters on poles as Tex had. "We didn't mean to hurt you."

"I know."

Sheridan tucked her bright yellow boots under the bench. As much as she wanted to unveil all of Elsie's secrets to the world, she realized it wasn't really up to her. Elsie had a right to tell her story her own way. As long as the girl was safe.

But what about Ribbon? Was Sheridan repeating the same mistake? "Elsie. Can I ask you a hard question?"

"I guess." The ten-year-old shrugged.

"Someone at my school died."

Elsie frowned.

Sheridan bit her lip and wondered how much she should say. But however infantile it seemed, she needed to hear from a victim whether or not her decision to tell Ribbon's story was fair. The last thing she wanted to do was continue the cycle of abuse.

"Her name was Ribbon. She was really cool, but nobody could see it."

"Why not?" Elsie shoulders relaxed.

Sheridan sensed the closeness return. "I don't know. Kids can be mean, you know, tease each other. Well, that made Ribbon really sad, but she didn't tell anyone. Instead, she wrote it all down in her journal."

"Was she afraid?"

"I think so. She's not here to ask, so I wonder what you think. Would it be bad for me to tell her story? You know, make sure the people who did it to her get punished?"

"Yes. I think Ribbon would be okay with that." Elsie tapped the heels of her tennis shoes together. "Besides, no one can tease her now."

Chapter 56

A shley dropped her animated fishing pole into the water on the television screen. The Wii Sport game didn't require any jumping or flailing of her hands. In fact, in order to win she had to do the opposite. Put the little hook by the fish's mouth and wait for it to grab on. It was the only video game she could beat Dad at.

A speckled fish with a trumpet nose bounced against her line, and her white handset vibrated. Ashley flipped back her wrist, and the fish popped out of the water, awarding her 250 points. Ashley pointed at the screen again and maneuvered her pole back into the cartoon pond. Dad would be home any time.

A small fish grabbed Ashley's line and pulled it around the pool a few times. Ashley didn't yank up because she knew the little fish would remove fifty points from her score. The back door slammed shut. Dad was home. He had told her on the phone that when he got back from the bank they needed to talk. She could only hope Courtney's dad wasn't part of the conversation.

Ashley turned off the game and went into the

kitchen. Dad wasn't there. Ashley looked out on the back porch and saw her father set a plastic bag on the patio table. The screen door slapped behind her, and she walked over to the lawn furniture.

"I bought Chinese food."

"Smells good."

Dad unpacked two Styrofoam containers from a Panda Express bag. "Orange chicken, fried rice, and two spring rolls for you."

"Perfect."

Ashley snapped the small chopsticks apart and picked up a piece of glazed meat. Dad settled across the table from her and forked a piece of broccoli. The silence between them was filled in by the rush of traffic on Sunset Cliffs Blvd. Palm trees and flowering shrubs blocked the view, but the hum of cars remained steady.

She wanted to tell Dad everything, but it was so hard. There were one hundred and one ways to say it, but not one of them wanted to leave her mouth. *Dad, I'm sorry. Dad, I'm horrible. Dad, I bullied my old friend to death.* All the words were swallowed with a bite of brown rice.

He sat across from her and studied everything to his left and to his right between bites. When he wasn't looking around the yard, he watched his food. Unspoken words seemed to trouble him.

"Do you want a drink?" Ashley asked.

"Just some water." Dad nodded.

Ashley went inside and filled two glasses from a gallon jug they kept in the fridge. When she got back to the table, Dad took a deep swig. He breathed out a contented sigh, then found the strength to push four words across his tongue and through his teeth. "It will be okay."

Dad said that when Mom first left. They'd lived in a small apartment in downtown San Diego. The carpet had fleas and the kitchen had roaches. But he had been right back then, and Ashley was convinced he was right today.

Chapter 57

Sheridan dropped her bag on the concrete stairs outside the school. What a ginormous waste of time. Her assembly at Oak Street High had been tolerable at best. The Northern California winter was equally lukewarm. She plopped down on the steps.

The *LA Times* article was sent over a week ago. The story was probably too little for that big city. Ribbon's story was stuck between Dullsville and the Emerald City. The phone in Sheridan's pocket vibrated. She pulled it out and checked the caller ID. Miss Shirley.

"Hello." Sheridan slumped over her knees.

"Hello, dear. I hope it went well. We'll talk about it as soon as I come get you. I'm just going to be a little late. Mrs. Olson needs me to stay another five or ten minutes. Her arthritis cripples her hands too much for her to get her laundry folded and put away. Poor thing. The dryer has another minute or so. Soon as I finish up this load I'll be over to get you. Are you okay to wait?"

"Fine."

"Great. I'll see you in a minute."

Sheridan clicked "end" on the phone. Really, Miss Shirley, where else would she go? The plan stunk. Sheridan rolled her phone around in her hand. Country kids were different. They knew how to make friends and keep them. When you only have a handful of other people your age to choose from, it was silly to make enemies of any of them. When kids get into arguments they pout a day or two, then get over it.

The San Diego school was so big you could make enemies with fifty people and still have dozens of others to choose from. City kids don't deal with drama. Instead, they store it up in hateful ways and throw it at each other.

Sheridan punched in a "Hey" to Tex on her phone. Maybe his assembly was more successful. He was probably in class, but she decided to try it anyway. She clicked send and leaned back on the school stairs. Of course, bullies lived in the country too. But they couldn't do as much damage. Teachers and janitors not only knew the parents—some them were the moms and dads.

The phone in her hand vibrated.

"Howdy," Tex sent.

Sheridan's thumbs bounced across the numeric pad, picking out letters. She didn't have a Blackberry like most kids, but she was learning the number-letter combinations. "How'd your Ribbon assembly go?"

Tex had been transferred to Orange County after the farm incident. His school was big. He could help get the word out much better than she could. A fly buzzed around her ear and she swatted at it.

"Haven't done it yet."

"Why not?"

"History. Biology. Stuff like that."

The pest hummed past her ear again, and she flailed her arms in frustration. Better to kill the insect than her brother. Was she the only one who cared about Ribbon? The fly landed on her arm and she smacked it with her open palm. The bug got away while her skin turned red where she'd slapped it.

Her phone vibrated again, and she glared at the screen.

"Just checking. Got to go, TTYL."

What was the point? The assembly was a dud. Her brother would rather do homework. Even the newspaper didn't care. At this rate she'd have kids of her own before anyone decided to do anything.

Miss Shirley's boat of a car pulled around the corner. Sheridan stood and dusted off the back of her pants. Might as well go back to the barn and graduate from home school. Miss Shirley would want a nap.

The car pulled up to the curb. Sheridan clomped down the steps and got in. Her antique foster mother pulled out in silent driver mode. The less conversation about how it went the better. The drive to the house would be about thirty minutes, but before Sheridan could settle into the seat, Miss Shirley pulled into the Dairy Queen.

People shouldn't be disappointed when it comes to ice cream, but Sheridan was. The detour meant conversation. She wasn't feeling it. "Why are we stopping here?"

Miss Shirley unbuckled her belt and smiled. "We're going to celebrate your grand achievement."

"Let's go home. The assembly was a flop."

"Come on, child, get out of the car. I've got a hankering for a Peanut Buster Parfait." The old lady got out of the car and headed for the entrance. "I know those nuts aren't good for my dentures, but sometimes you've got to live it up."

Sheridan pushed open the heavy door. Why should Miss Shirley listen? No one else did. Inside, she ordered an ice cream sandwich and sat on a hard plastic chair.

"Now, who stole your smile? Cheer up. You look like you could stand some good news."

"Why? You got some?" Sheridan wrapped a napkin around her chocolate sandwich.

"Yup." Miss Shirley stabbed her spoon into the mixture of ice cream and hot fudge. "Have you ever heard of Dr. Woods?"

"Who hasn't?" Sheridan licked the edge of her sandwich. "He's that former comedian turned talk-show host."

"Right." Miss Shirley scooped out a messy bit of her soft serve. "Well, he's more than just a funny face. He's got what you call 'skills.'"

"I guess." Sheridan bit into the chocolate layered sandwich. "Didn't he get his degree in sociology or something like that?"

"His doctorate." Miss Shirley beamed with pride. "You remind me of him sometimes. Your tenaciousness. Comedy always came natural to him, but he never wanted that to be his only purpose in life. If you've seen his show, he's not much for the sensationalized baby-momma drama. Nope. He's always wanted to cover cutting-edge topics. Change the world and all."

"You know Dr. Woods?"

"He was one of my boys." Miss Shirley licked the end of her tall spoon. "I shouldn't say *was*. All of them are my kids forever." Hot fudge dripped down the side of the plastic container. Miss Shirley curled it on the spoon like spaghetti.

Sheridan shook her head. No way. This old lady actually knew the most famous talk-show host on daytime TV? Sheridan rested her hand on the table, making sure her ice cream didn't touch the surface. The day had been filled with disappointment and Sheridan didn't dare hope. That's why she had to ask Miss Shirley to repeat herself when she asked, "Do you want to be on his show?"

"You're kidding."

"Why would I do that?" Miss Shirley scrunched her nose. "This whole business about bullies is important. I told you before that I think kids in public school get away with too much these days. The government has taken away the power from the teachers. And parents today would rather be friends with their kids than instill a little respect and discipline. Maybe we need to rely on the next generation to effect change."

A drop of ice cream plopped onto the table. Sheridan lifted the melting sandwich to her mouth and licked the circumference. The Dr. Woods show was nationwide. Forget about her vision of reaching the kids in San Diego or Orange County. This opportunity could reach to every inner city in the United States and Canada. As far as she knew, it might even be shown in other countries as well.

"Why didn't you tell me before?" Sheridan ran around the small table and hugged Miss Shirley.

"I needed to see if you were serious." The old lady smiled and straightened her blouse. "What kind of mother would I be if I ran to Jimmy with every little whim I've heard? No. I needed to see if you would go through with it. And you did. You wrote to the papers and held your assembly. Besides, as much as I like to brag on my children, I try to keep silent about the famous ones."

"You have more than one?"

"I don't like to brag." Miss Shirley tipped her head to the side. "I'll tell you what. Jimmy was always a bit of a rascal." She chuckled. "He used to keep me in stitches with his jokes."

"I can't believe you call him Jimmy."

"What else would I call him? That's his name. Makes no never mind to me if he has one fan or a million. As long as he's doing the right thing."

Sheridan nodded.

"Most folks these days say they want their kids to be happy. Not me. Happiness for one person can lead to pain in another. Nope. I've always said I want my kids to do something with their lives. Put the other guy first. You know, live a humble life. Not one full of what can I get. Too much of that going on. Life is better when you give."

The idea touched something honest inside Sheridan. The media labeled today's kids the "Me Generation." She hated it. She didn't care about getting famous as much as she wanted to make life better for someone else.

Chapter 58

Ashley propped her camera on the driver's side window. Through the lens she spotted the bench where she last saw Ribbon alive. She adjusted the zoom and tried her best to make sure she had the same angle. The black-and-white copy of her former friend's photo lay on the seat next to her. She glanced back and forth at it and the viewfinder.

She imagined the end result in the school yearbook. Two photos side by side. One with the profile of a pensive Ribbon, the other of an empty bench. The message would be subtle, yet honorary at the same time. The yearbook teacher would never hear her idea unless Professor Barber or his wife said it was okay. This was an exercise in hope.

With one last glance, Ashley clicked off a couple of shots. A butterfly bounced across the sky. Its uneven flight appeared dependent on the wind. It took a minute before Ashley could follow it through the camera's lens. The wings weren't a vibrant color. Instead, their black and white, zebra-like stripes were a beautiful contrast against the blue sky. She clicked a couple of shots. It was odd to think how those graceful wings came from a creepy caterpillar. Her mood had changed much over the last month.

A couple weeks ago she'd gotten a beat down from the gang outside this very church. Before she could become too philosophical, her phone rang. The ringtone indicated it was Dad. She wasn't expected home yet. School only got out a few minutes ago.

"Hello." Ashley set the camera on the back seat and started the ignition.

"Hey, are you on your way home?"

"Yeah, I'm leaving now."

"Well, stop by the Barbers first, will you? Professor Barber called and he needs to talk to you."

"Okay." Thoughts of the butterfly flitted from her mind to her stomach. "Is something wrong?"

"I don't think so. Go on over there and then call me before you head home."

"Sure." The professor hadn't spoken to Ashley the entire time she'd worked in his backyard.

She pulled out into the road. The loud blare of a horn behind her forced her to slam on her brakes. The photo of Ribbon on the church bench slipped to the passenger floorboard, and her camera landed with a thud on the back floorboard. Yikes. That was close. She needed to focus on driving.

A boy in a red sports car whipped around her and flipped his middle finger at her. Great. She gripped the wheel and waited for her pulse to slow down. It was her fault; she didn't even look. A car accident wouldn't be a good thing right now. Whatever Professor Barber had in store for her, it wouldn't be as bad as wrecking her car.

Ashley checked her mirror and looked over her shoulder a couple of times before pulling away from the curb. She tried to stay focused on the road, but the thought of an angry father loomed at her future destination. What could he want? It definitely wouldn't be good, whatever it was.

The light at the intersection changed from green to yellow. Ashley pressed hard on her brakes. Traffic crisscrossed the intersection. Except for her, everyone was in a hurry to get someplace.

The light changed and she pulled into the neighborhood. On the corner, the pinkie-ring-bartering flower lady sat in a lawn chair, waiting for customers. Two lefts and a right brought her to the Barbers' cul-de-sac. Ribbon's father sat on the porch, waiting for her. His stoic face provided no clue as to what he wanted to say. His eyes stayed focused on the sky as she approached.

"Hello." Ashley pulled open the gate. "My dad said you wanted to see me."

The man nodded without looking her way. She climbed the steps and waited. It felt odd standing over him, but she didn't want to sit without being invited.

"I got a call from a reporter the other day."

Oh, great. "Sir, I didn't tell anyone."

"Who said you did?"

"No one." She didn't expect him to be friendly.

"Well, I turned them down. I'm not interested in having Ribbon's life dissected and misquoted in the press."

Ashley hugged one of the posts holding up the porch awning. A part of her brain lied and said it wasn't her fault, while the truthful side said everything that happened was her fault. It was all connected to her.

"I got another call today," he said.

"I'm sorry." And she was, very sorry.

"It wasn't from the *Times*. It was a producer from the Dr. Woods show."

"What?" Ashley's knees rocked. No way.

"They wanted to confirm some facts about my daughter's death."

That was crazy impossible. "How did Dr. Woods find out about Ribbon?"

"I don't know." Professor Barber propped his elbow on the arm of the swing. "I've given them permission to tell Ribbon's story."

"Excuse me?" It was hard to breathe. Pandora's box had nothing on the mess that lay in store for this family. "I don't think that's a good idea."

"Oh, really?" The man glared at her. "Aren't you the one who was gung ho to go to the police? You were the one with all the facts."

"Yes, but..."

"But nothing. The producer made some very good points. There's a girl in Yuba County that somehow got Ribbon's journal and, well, she wants to honor my daughter's life. Seems a bunch of bullies had been tormenting my daughter for years."

Tinkerbell. Ashley stared at her shoes.

"Oh, yeah, that's right." He leaned back in the chair. "The little drama fit you threw on the steps the other day. Well, maybe you'll get your chance to see the inside of a jail cell. Seems you were a big part of Ribbon's misery. Now you get to go public. Now you get to tell your story to more than the police."

"This isn't about me."

"You better believe it." He pushed the swing hard. It

bounced against the house.

"But I thought you didn't want to exploit..."

"Don't tell me what I do or don't want. You know nothing about me. And it appears you know nothing about my daughter. Ribbon would have wanted this. She would have wanted her life to mean something. This girl, Sheridan, wants to make sure my daughter's death isn't in vain."

"You don't know that."

"Really?" He didn't blink. His stare penetrated Ashley's defenses. Then he spoke the words she thought. "Who are you to decide what's best for Ribbon? You may have my wife fooled. But I'm not so blind." He stood up.

The weeds in the overgrown front yard trembled in the wind. Ashley's punishment was about to go nationwide. She didn't want the coward in her to win, but she was scared. The idea of running away, disappearing into a world that didn't know her poked the back of her mind. But she was done hiding. She'd been circling her life the way a dog chases his tail. "I'll do whatever you want me to do."

Chapter 59

"Welcome to the show."

Sheridan melted. Part of the reason the world adored Dr. Woods was because he was hot. The tall black man had perfect features, an intoxicating smile with a gorgeous voice to match. Smooth like soft butter. But what Sheridan discovered in meeting him face-to-face was the deep sincerity in his eyes. Compassion and honesty were truly attractive.

"Have you ever been on TV before?"

"No." She faced the mirror in the make-up room.

"Don't be nervous." Dr. Woods patted her shoulder. "You'll be fine."

"Thanks." Sheridan didn't want to pinch herself in front of the makeup artist. Stuff like this never happened to foster kids or troublemakers. The skinny redhead winked at her, then finished applying a heavy coat of foundation on her face.

"Close your eyes."

A soft brush stroked her cheek. The thick powder covered every one of Sheridan's external flaws. How had she come so far? The idea that a throw-away like her was sitting in a chair that had been occupied by celebrities was sublime. As a person who most wanted to fade from the world's microscope, her image was about to be cast into outer space, bounced off a distant satellite and stretched out of proportion on millions of flat screens.

"So, what brings you to the show?"

"I've come to tell someone else's story."

"That's cool. Open your eyes." The woman studied Sheridan's face. "Look up." With soft strokes she applied mascara. "What's your friend's story?"

"She killed herself because of bullies."

"Wow. That's really sad." The makeup artist's tone didn't change as she set down the eye make-up and grabbed some blush. "Suck in your cheeks and pucker."

Sheridan was glad she couldn't speak for the moment. The lady's bland attitude at hearing someone died reminded Sheridan she was on a talk show. These people were all about getting ratings. And now she'd become part of it.

She wiped her hands on her pant legs a couple of times. There wasn't any magic chant that could ensure she'd be protected from unfair edits. Had she made a mistake? Ribbon was dead. The girl could never be her friend. Not today or tomorrow. Was she about to make it worse?

"Okay. Now open your mouth into an oval." A light coat of lipstick and gloss were applied before the woman spun the chair back toward the mirror. "How's that?"

"Fine." Sheridan didn't care that the word came out hard.

"Don't be nervous. You'll be okay."

"Do you think I'm here for me?"

The artist's head jerked back in reflex.

"A real girl is dead." Sheridan pulled off the plastic bib they'd given her. "I'm here to tell people why. You probably meet all kinds of famous people or hear hundreds of sad stories. But I'm not here to turn Ribbon's story into idle small talk."

"No problem." The lady shrugged. Sheridan had hit a nerve.

"Thank you for the makeup. Can I go back to the greenroom now?"

"Yes, we're done."

"Great." Sheridan flexed the muscles in her arms. Glad the fight had returned to her spirit. It was stupid to get all gaga over Dr. Woods.

The desensitized crew was only a means to an end. She needed to stay cool and focused.

"You look beautiful." Nina smiled at her. Miss Shirley didn't want to make the commute to Los Angeles, but it was only two hours from San Diego. "Are you ready to do this?"

"More than ever."

In the room were two other people: an author who'd written a book on cyber-bullies and a nice couple who started a movement after their son died of suicide.

A bald man with a headset poked his face into the room. "Watch the monitor. The show's about to begin. I'll be back to bring you to the stage when we get close."

Everyone said okay.

Sheridan leaned forward in her seat. Nerves had been replaced with adrenaline. *Let's do this.* Dr. Woods' image came through the set in the greenroom. There was no difference between what she saw here and what Miss Shirley would be watching at home. Except it wouldn't air for a couple days.

"On today's show, we're going to cover two topics." The former comedian stood with his hand on a mic. "Bullying and suicide." He had beat Oprah in the ratings the last year she was on the air.

The headset guy came into the room. "Mr. Kroux, you're first. Come with me."

The author left the room with his book clenched in his palm. Dr. Woods spoke about the connection while newspaper articles shifted across the TV screen. "It's become an epidemic."

The tips of Sheridan's fingers felt frozen. She shook them as hard as she could, then stood and paced the room. The couple whose son had committed suicide smiled up at her. No one said anything. They stewed in their frayed nerves together.

The man with the headset came and got Sheridan next. He took her down a long hallway. Sheridan heard the studio audience on the other side of the partition.

"Just like we practiced," the man whispered. "As soon as you hear your name, go around to the stage."

"Sure." The words barely exited her mouth. She cleared her throat.

"I'm going to cue your mic, so don't say anything you don't want millions of people to hear."

Sheridan nodded and wiped her cold hands together, trying to restore circulation. Then she heard it.

"Please welcome Sheridan Alexander to the show."

That was her signal. Her feet hiccupped once before she found her balance and entered the stage. The lights were blinding. Sheridan shook her hands and moved toward the seat next to Dr. Woods. In rehearsal, the auditorium-styled chairs facing the stage had been empty. Now she could make out the movement of people in the audience. Joe was out there somewhere. He drove up from San Diego with Nina.

"Thank you so much for coming." Dr. Woods' hand was warm as she shook it.

"Thanks for having me."

"Ladies and gentlemen. What's fascinating about this young lady is while she's led an interesting life, she's not here to tell her story, but to speak for someone who can no longer do it herself."

So far, so good. Sheridan acknowledged the applause with a small nod and kept her focus on the kind-brown eyes of Dr. Woods. He led her through the conversation with questions she knew how to answer. The minutes passed as she spoke about locker 572, Ribbon's journal, and eventually the campaign.

"If you could tell other high school kids how to help, what would you say?" He pointed to the camera to the left of the stage.

"Do something. Start today. Wear a ribbon. I'm even talking to the guys. You can tie a blue or red ribbon to the zipper on your backpack. I'm asking everyone to wear a ribbon to show they are against bullying."

"How will people know the ribbons symbolize an end to bullying?" Dr. Woods leaned toward her. "Some kids might use ribbons without intending to be against bullying."

"That's okay." She looked back at the host. It was much easier talking to him than the one-eyed inanimate object representing the world. "The ribbon's meant to be a reminder more than anything else."

"I don't understand." Dr. Woods relaxed in his seat. This wasn't rehearsed. He warned her before the show his questions might lead them down an unpracticed path.

She blew out a breath and thought a minute. "Have you ever had someone smile at you by accident?" Sheridan leaned her arm on the chair and erased the audience from her mind.

"Sure."

"How did it make you feel?"

"Good." The talk show host chuckled. He didn't seem to mind having the questions turned on him for a change.

"Even though the smile wasn't intended for you, it still felt good."

"Of course."

"The ribbons are like a smile, a simple reminder of kindness. At some point I hope everyone will wear them to send a message. That's why I'm on your show." She faced the big-lens camera. "Let's let the bullies know it's over." Sheridan faced Dr. Woods again. "I think most kids in school don't like the people who pick fights and shove others around, slam them up against walls, gang up on them in the restrooms, do wedgies, call them names in the halls or on the Internet. But nobody knows how to stop it."

"I think you're right," the host agreed.

"The majority of people are good and decent; they only act like a helpless minority. Well, let's flip that. Send a message with a ribbon of any color and bring the unconnected majority together."

"Sheridan has the right idea," the book writer chimed in. "Too many kids try to seek vengeance on their own. The truth is many people who try to stop bullies end up becoming bullies themselves."

Sheridan bit the inside of her cheek. Her conversation with Elsie tugged at her. She'd joined the bullies in the ring. But fighting them leaves everyone bruised, and no one ever achieves anything.

"Some people on the Internet actually think they are helping by picking up the hate and throwing it right back at their enemies," she said.

The station manager was signaling a break.

"Not a good idea." Dr. Woods faced the camera. "When we come back, I have a surprise for Sheridan." The talk-show host winked at her. "We'll be right back."

Chapter 60

"Ashley, are you there?" The words came through the small headset she wore in the school basement. Dr. Woods' mobile camera crew had warned Ashley about the camera's red light. Now that it shone bright, the world could see everything she did. "Can you tell us your connection to this story?"

She cleared her throat.

"Ribbon was my best friend until sixth grade. In junior high, I let her down. I picked being popular over being loyal. I can never take back the horrible things I did, but I'm trying to make sure they never happen again."

Ashley stepped out of the way of the camera. Locker 572 was covered in daisies, cards, balloons, and stuffed animals. The crew sent in a couple of kids. The janitor walked over and dropped a bouquet of daisies on the pile of flowers near the floor of the locker, while another girl tied a pink balloon to the dozen that were already there.

"Can you tell us what we are seeing?"

"It's a tribute to Ribbon. Everyone at North Harbor wants the bullies to stop."

"Does that mean you've given up your participation?"

"Yes, sir. I can never replace Ribbon. But I can stop being part of the problem."

The TV crew put a monitor across from the camera. Ashley watched Tinkerbell touch a handkerchief to her eyes. "They're trying to fix it. Only, they did it better than me. Look at that. It's beautiful." The moment nagged a tear from Ashley.

"Thank you, ladies." Dr. Woods' face filled the screen. "We'll be right back."

The cameraman gave Ashley the cue, and the red light went off.

She stepped away while the crew prepared to record another angle of the lockers at the end of the break.

Miss Jones sat on the floor in the wider basement hallway. Her bohemian skirt covered her crossed legs. She craned her neck and looked up as Ashley approached. "You did good."

"Thanks."

"No problem." The counselor shrugged.

"No, really." Ashley squatted so her eyes were level with Miss Jones. "Thanks. If it wasn't for you, none of this would be possible."

"I appreciate that. People used to laugh at my paper hoarding. But when it comes down to it, each piece of paper in my office represents a person. They're all important."

"Copies of your reports were enough to get Courtney's father in a lot of trouble," Ashley acknowledged.

"The man should never have tried to get me fired."

"You probably saved my dad's job as well."

"It helped a lot that you went to the police. They were ready for all my paperwork."

Ashley smiled. Miss Jones probably didn't know the real reason Ashley had gone to the police. None of that mattered anymore. "Tinkerbell's right."

"Who's Tinkerbell?"

"That girl on the show." Ashley pointed toward the camera.

"Oh, you mean Sheridan."

"Yeah. Sheridan. Courtney might have a crust as thick as the earth, and then wreak havoc on innocent villages like a volcano, but she's just trying to make it like the rest of us."

The cameraman came back over. "You ready to go back on the air?"

"Yes." Ashley got up and walked back to locker 572. The fresh aroma of daises overpowered the waxy smell of high school.

Chapter 61

"No man is an island." That's my mother's favorite quote. In her environmental opinion it connects every person's actions to their effects on the earth. But these days I wonder. What if my parents got it wrong? Maybe it's more about people than the planet.

Kids at school do whatever they want because they are only hurting themselves. But is that really true? Do the opinions of one person ripple across a sea of others and touch an entire society? That seems to be true in my life. The judgments of Courtney and her cronies have become high school facts. Even to me.

Well, I found another John Donne quote: "All mankind is of one author, and is one volume; when one man dies, one chapter is not torn out of the book, but translated into a better language; and every chapter must be so translated."

A better language. I like that. Let someone else fill the page, I'm too tired. If anyone's life needs to be shredded and recycled, mine does. The world would be a whole lot better if I was no longer in it.

Chapter 62

The show was over. Sheridan took a drink of water. The girl on the big screen had looked familiar, but Sheridan couldn't place her. But none of that mattered now. The world had become different for her. She unclipped her mic and gave it to the bald headset guy.

"You know, Dr. Woods, I don't think Ribbon wanted to die."

Dr. Woods nodded as the crew took his equipment. "Probably not."

"But she didn't want to live either. Not with the pain." Sheridan hopped out of the chair. "But Ribbon got it wrong."

"Of course she did." The host rested his hand on her shoulder. "She left the game at half-time because her team was behind. She missed the most amazing comeback in her life."

"Death should never be someone's goal."

"Definitely." Dr. Woods smiled. "We're all born for a reason. Ma Shirley taught me that." The host crossed his arms over his chest. His show was dedicated to this concept of meaning and purpose in every life. "I read Ribbon's whole journal, you know, before the show. Research. She misunderstood the John Donne chapter quote. He was talking about the connection of purpose to people." The handsome man coughed a little, lifted his hand, and said in a Shakespearian voice, "'Ask not for whom the bell tolls; it tolls for thee.' Or something like that." He laughed. "Look it up later."

"I will."

The cameraman moved some equipment around. The crew adjusted lights for the next show and rolled away two of the chairs from the stage.

"I think John Donne wanted something bigger for people. You know, folks need to be less focused on their personal desires and more on the needs of an entire society. Too many people like to ask, 'Why doesn't anybody do something about it?' I know I was one of them. I think he hoped people would start asking 'What can I do?'" He shrugged. "I've got to get ready for my next guest."

"Of course."

"Give Ma Shirley a big hug for me."

Sheridan joined Nina and Joe in the greenroom. It contained a few new faces. The mother of the bullied boy came over and shook Sheridan's hand. "Good job."

"Thanks." Sheridan stood and straightened her skirt.

"By the way, I love the boots."

Sheridan bounced on the balls of her feet. As a short person, she preferred tall shoes. The little bit of leather and a three-inch heel weren't as flashy as Dorothy's red slippers, but she couldn't help but click her heels together.

"Let's go home."

From the Author

In my research, I've discovered many really smart kids consider suicide. While ideas of death cloud their minds, they often express a conflicting message, "I don't want to live, but I don't want to die either."

The Center for Disease Control conducted a survey across the United States[1]. The data indicated 12% of youth deaths happen because of suicide. That means if ten kids you know died, at least one of them chose to do it. In addition, the CDC questioned high school students about health and behavior in 39 states and 22 locals:

- 14.5% seriously considered suicide. In your next English class, count fourteen random kids. At least two have seriously found life too painful to endure.
- 11% have a suicide plan. The next time you are at the movies, find ten teens. One of them has probably thought enough about death to plan how they would do it.
- 6.9% admitted to attempted suicide. Look through your school yearbook and find thirty faces; two of those people have actually tried to kill themselves.

The possibility you are part of these numbers is not unrealistic. The world can be a harsh place. Other people's words can twist our own thoughts into self-doubt. Before you listen, even to yourself, get a second opinion. Talk to someone, anyone. There's a free, anonymous hotline where you can ask questions and discuss your experiences. Whether it's about bullying or thoughts of suicide. Call 1 - 800-273-TALK.

---

[1] CDC, 2007 Youth Risk Behavior Surveillance System

Acknowledgments

I want to thank **YOU**, the person holding this book in your hands. Usually acknowledgments are written to the many people in the production production of a book, (listed below). However, the real reason this book has reached a fourth edition is because people like you have read it end to end.

Thank you to my fans, for those who not only told their friends, but have gone out to Amazon, Goodreads or other sources and rated this book. It might not seem like a big, thing, but it enables others to find quality books. If you haven't rated this book, please do. Your support doesn't go unnoticed.

Thanks also to those who participated in the long and successful journey this book has taken:

- God, for his love, and my husband, Claude, for his prayers.
- My early readers and first-draft editors, my daughters, Ariel and Langston. Friends who read this book, Cathy Ater, Bruce Butler, and Nolong Abbey.
- The experts who believed in me and helped me polish my craft: Randy Ingermanson, Bob Irvin, Jim Bell, Donald Maas, Mary DeMuth, Trisha Goyer, Karen Ball, and Julie Gwinn.
- Critique groups members, Ginny Smith, Marcia Hornok, Jim Thatcher, and Jim Cook, Bob Kaku, Lynda Quinn, Carrie Padgett, Christen Morris, Leslee Clapp, Sarah Phillip, and Becky Loescher.
- The professionals: Sergeant Rand Padgett, retired from the Clovis, CA, police department. Jeni Gudac, high school guidance counselor. Myra Thomas, tenured social worker.
- The Cover Collection for the fourth edition cover as well as those on the next page.

Without one of these many links, the chain making up this book would have been broken.

What's Next?

Do you wonder what happened to Courtney?

Get a glimpse into the consequences of her mean-girl behavior in *The Center Trilogy.*

Hidden high in the Rocky Mountains, The Center houses inmates ages 12 to 22. The experiment in reform isn't without controversy. Blogs report students being tasered or tortured in a dungeon. 18-year-old Courtney doesn't buy the hype; concentration-camp tactics wouldn't fly in America, especially not for the niece of a US Senator. Right?

Will Courtney find a way to run things on the inside the way she did on the outside? Or will The Center take away more than her freedom?

Turn the page and read the first chapter for yourself.

CHAPTER 1

"The question isn't who is going to let me..."

Love sucks!

It kicks your butt, breaks your heart, and gets you hand-cuffed in an airplane headed to hell. I drop my head against the seat in front of me. Thanks to my ridiculous parents and a stupid judge, I get to finish high school at The Center.

Big smile.

Not.

No more Pep rallies or proms. It's the middle of May and I should be at Saks buying shoes to make my graduation gown less boring, not headed to god-forsaken Grand Junction, freaking, Colorado. Lifting my chin, I stare out the small window and act as if I'm cool with the metal bracelets. Pretend I'm gaining street cred or headed to some Orange-Is-the-New-Black experience. Trying hard to fool even myself. The shiver in my bones isn't from the cold, I'm actually scared. The Manchester fortune purchased my way into what my mother, calls a "reform school", but internet stories make The Center sound like a contemporary concentration camp.

Students Tasered.

Inmates deprogrammed in a dungeon.

I don't want to believe it. I tell myself it's all hype. Colorado is in America. My family is not only wealthy, we're politically connected. A school for troubled, rich kids will be monitored. Constantly monitored. No one could get away with torture.

The plane bounces on its decline, stirring up the airline pretzels I ate on the previous flight. Man, I feel sick. The chemical funk of recirculated air hurts my head. I tap my blue stilettos in the nonexistent legroom. I might have to go to jail, but I want to do it in style, and public puking isn't cool. The small, wannabe plane twists at random angles as it encounters turbulence.

Ping.

The fasten-your-seatbelt sign illuminates.

The officer sitting next to me doesn't move, so neither do I. He thinks he's in control because of his gun. My stomach begs to differ.

Bounce.

Oh, no.

Thump.

Don't puke, Courtney. Do not puke.

With my wrists cuffed, I press my hand on my gut to fight back the nausea. I've been in a lot of messes before but nothing quite as big as this. My parents accuse me of trampling over anything to be seen or heard. School counselors say I have an overwhelming need to be validated. They're all nuts if they think I wanted this.

The plane rocks and bounces toward the runway. A layer of snow dusts the mountain range below. Not good. Most of my life was spent near the ocean in San Diego where it never snows. But living near DC for the last year, I learned that fast wheels don't work on icy surfaces. I brace myself for impact.

Metal cuts into my wrists as I squeeze my hands together. I'm not the kind of person who regrets much, but man do I hate every minute I spent in Virginia. I hate that my father made us leave San Diego. I hate Daniel. I hate Nicole. I hate my cousin Bailey. I might have messed up. But I didn't mess up alone. One thing is for sure, I will NEVER fall in love again.

With a bump, the back wheels of the plane grab tarmac.

I hold my breath and wait for us to spin out of control and smash into the side of a mountain. Good-bye life.

The front wheels drop.

I clench my jaw and tighten my shoulders. I don't know the best position for a plane crash. Who watches stupid safety demonstrations?

The brakes skid.

The wheels roll.

No spinning. I brave a look from the window. To my surprise the runway is dry. Snow still tops the mountains, but the airport looks like spring. Good-bye life.

"You okay?" the officer asks.

"Yeah," I say a little bit snarky.

He chuckles. "Just checking. Thought I heard you say something like 'good-bye life'."

I clench my teeth and watch the barren landscape as the airplane bounces across the tarmac. I hate it when words fall from my brain through my lips without me being fully aware of it. "Whatever." I feel more disappointed than embarrassed. Who cares what some dumb cop thinks of me? Besides, I think I kind of wanted to have my life end in a ball of flames. I'd be famous, in viral videos and twitter hashtags. A thousand times better than vomiting in a bag. Plus, my mother and father would be forced to regret their decision to send me here.

Mother claimed, "You'll come out a better person."

Father said, "It's for the best."

I don't believe them. If my little sister was in trouble, they'd have saved her this humiliation. But they love her more. They really do. It happens.

The evidence was presented to me at a very young age. The sun had shown bright through the park trees. With my fingers in a wide begging motion, I reached for my father to pick me up and swing me. His face disappeared as he stepped into the shade and shook his head. He claimed it was not safe. That was my first experience of rejection's heaviness. I tried to believe him. But his lie became evident the minute Kat was born. My sister and biggest rival.

He swung her around as a baby.

He swings her around now and she's ten.

Swinging equals love.

No swinging.

No love.

No big. Turns out swinging only makes me vomit. Even watching a merry-go-round makes me dizzy. I push the spinning memories from my mind and take a couple deep breaths to quell the returning nausea.

When the plane comes to a full stop, I press my forehead against the seat in front of me. The flight attendant announces we can unbuckle our seat belts, but since the officer next to me doesn't move, neither do I.

It's good not to move. Stay still. Not vomit.

I could sit here and wonder what I should have done differently, but the list would be too long. Besides, I haven't done anything everyone isn't already doing. I don't see them here.

The officer stands. I lift my head and see that the small plane has emptied. I slide to the aisle. The cop leaves me shackled while we exit. The flight attendant stuffs my coat in the gap between my arm and my side. Her hands shake as if I'm a bank robber or a murderer.

"Can't you take these off?" I lift my wrists while continuing to glare at the stupid flight attendant.

"Nope," the cop says without a smile. If he were better looking I'd consider flirting my way out. But seeing how he reminds me of the Grinch, I think I'll pass. He stands close enough to grab me if I run. Trigger hand clenches, ready for the challenge. He can relax. I'm not a runner. That's not my style.

Neither is throwing up, so I snatch a gulp of air, hold it in my lungs until it fights for release. With my shoulders thrown back, I exhale and strut through the small terminal. The heels of my blue Louboutin's click on the tile floor. The officer pulls my bright pink carry-on bag behind him. I smile at the odd looks he gets. A little humiliation back at him.

People stare at me too. A mother yanks her small child away after I wave at him with my two hands clasped in shiny bracelets. The reaction widens my smile. I'm tempted to whisper to them, want to know who I killed and the bank I robbed?

"Excuse me?" The officer asks.

"Nothing." Ugh, lousy slips. My mouth totally hates me. I keep my eyes forward and bite my bottom lip. No more teasing the nice Colorado people.

When the sliding glass doors open, the crisp, mid-morning air dispels more of my "green gills" as Nanny Bella would say with her thick Mexican accent. I fill both my lungs with spring air as I remember my plump caretaker. We walk across the parking lot and I'm surprised to find the bright sun warms my cheeks, different from the bitter bite of wind they have in Virginia.

In fact, I'm surprised at the sun's warmth, considering it's spring. The comfortable temperature mocks the mountain snow. I inhale again. The smell of burnt wood lingers in my nostrils. It helps. On carnival rides, I yell at the top of my lungs to keep the nausea down. Not wanting to cry out, I pull in air through a wide-open mouth.

One thing for sure, when this trip is over, I'll be the best person ever. I never want to be this humiliated again. My pathetic search for love got me into this mess. But I'm done with men. No one needs that nonsense.

Of course, that's easy to say, harder to do when my new guard appears.

Holy hot.

He leans against the ugliest, green school bus on the planet. Which only makes him hotter. His blue-gray eyes twinkle with mystery. His hair hangs in long waves like a Greek god. Lord knows I have a weakness for older men.

Butterflies or bats awaken in my already sick stomach.

"Jackson, this is Courtney Manchester." The stern officer passes my pink bag to the guard. Unlike the cop next to me, the Adonis who takes my carry-on wears a uniform that fits tight against his athletic frame.

I offer a weak smile.

"Hi." He dazzles one right back at me. A single, infuriatingly gorgeous dimple sinks into his right cheek.

Jerk.

My desire to not vomit escalates. I suddenly regret not throwing up in the terminal. I want nothing left in my stomach to embarrass me in front of this guy. I suck in more air, step onto the bus, and into the cage separating the driver from the riders. The exquisite guard follows.

The seats aren't empty. Three kids sit, scattered on board. In the center of the back row, a tattooed jock glares at me, his leg chained to the floor. Four seats in front of him, a short Latino guy stares out the window, a Bose headset wrapped around his neck. Nearer the front, a young black girl wipes her red, swollen eyes.

I smile at her in spite of myself. I don't believe in people. They only betray you, but for some reason I feel sorry for this sad girl. If I can do anything in the next few minutes to make her life a bit brighter, then maybe I'll shift some of that karma stuff people talk about.

"I'm Courtney." I nod at her.

"Dee Dee." She lifts her shoulders in a shy shrug.

I slide into the seat across from her. The vinyl is hot on my bottom. Jackson leans over and removes my "jewelry." His breath warm on my neck. A moment that could have been über romantic if it wasn't for his toxic cologne. The musky smell would have been great on any other stomach day, but today I plug my nose waiting for him to shackle me to the floor like the kid in back.

But, he pockets the cuffs and leaves me unrestrained. The gate at the front of the bus clicks closed. The guard is gone. I shake my head and scoot closer to the window searching for oxygen.

"Look, Ángel, a blond princess," the jock in the back heckles in a thick Southern accent. "They didn't tie her leg down either. Guess they trust these heifers more than us."

"Shut up, Fisher."

"Make me!"

The conversation happens behind me. I'm too nauseous to turn around. But I can respond and do. With my right hand still gripping the seat in front of me, I flash the middle finger of my left hand to everyone behind me.

"You'll pay for that, princess," Fisher growls. "Soon as I get a shank, I'm gonna gut you."

I don't answer. Can't answer. Not because he scares me—I can handle a creep like him. No, if I open my mouth, I'll lose my lunch. The nausea pushes hard against my ribs. No amount of deep breathing works. The walls of the bus narrow. The air thickens.

Hot.

Heavy.

Staring at the seat in front of me, I beg the green vinyl to make the pressure stop. But it doesn't work. Instead, I open my mouth as wide as possible and scream.

Coming Soon

Oh my gosh, I'm so grateful to you for reading my book. It's an honor to have someone read the last page. Please check out the link below, **subscribe to my website and I will send you a free eBook copy of** *The Center*

www.kodzoBooks.com

Maybe you are already a fan. Maybe you have already subscribed. Maybe you don't like subscribing to email lists (I promise mine will not spam your inbox, I spend more of my time working on books than sending emails. Mostly I like to tell fans about other free book offers, unique fan offerings, or periodically let them know what I'm working on or ask for input on my work in progress, etc).

Either way, I still want to offer you a deal **The compilation for all three books will be 50% off the price of buying each individual novel.**